# PICTURE OF INNOCENCE

## JACQUELINE BAIRD

~ ITALIAN TEMPTATION! ~

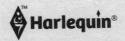

TORONTO NEW YORK LONDON
AMSTERDAM PARIS SYDNEY HAMBURG
STOCKHOLM ATHENS TOKYO MILAN MADRID
PRAGUE WARSAW BUDAPEST AUCKLAND

Recycling programs for this product may not exist in your area.

ISBN-13: 978-0-373-52809-7

PICTURE OF INNOCENCE

First North American Publication 2011

# PICTURE OF INNOCENCE

# CHAPTER ONE

LORENZO ZANELLI, owner of the centuries-old Zanelli Merchant Bank, originally bankers to Italian principalities and now a global concern, exited the elevator at his office suite on the top floor of the magnificent old building in the heart of Verona, a frown marring his broad brow.

His business lunch with Manuel Cervantes, the head of an Argentinean conglomerate whose family had been valued clients for years, had gone well, but Lorenzo was not a happy man... His secretary had called to warn him he was going to be late for his next appointment as his lunch had severely overrun—despite the fact that they had completed their business quite quickly.

As soon as work was out of the way Manuel had turned to a more personal topic: the necessity of giving up his career as a mountaineer and keen photographer to take over the running of the company after the death of his father five years ago and his subsequent marriage and two children. Then finally he had shown Lorenzo some shots he had belatedly got around to printing from his last trip to the Alps.

They were pictures taken at the main base camp on Manuel's final expedition to Mont Blanc, and included by sheer chance a few shots of Lorenzo's brother,

Antonio, and Damien Steadman his friend, wearing bright red jackets and even brighter grins, just arriving as Manuel's team were about to start their ascent.

The next morning Manuel's team had been on the last stage of the climb to the summit when he had received news that his father had suffered a heart attack. He'd been airlifted off the mountain by helicopter, and his last shot was a view of the mountain as he was flown down to base camp for the dash back to Argentina to be at his father's bedside. He had heard much later of Antonio's tragic death, and had thought Lorenzo would like to have what were probably the last pictures of his brother. Lorenzo was grateful, but it brought back memories he had spent years trying to forget.

Lorenzo had been looking through the photos as he'd walked back to his offices, taking in the implications of the detail in the landscape shot Manuel had pointed out to him, when he'd literally bumped into an old friend, Olivia Paglia, which had delayed him even further.

His frown deepened as he saw the fair head of a woman seated in the reception area, obviously waiting for him. He had almost forgotten about Miss Steadman, and now was not the best time to deal with her...

'Lucy Steadman?' he queried, casting a dark glance her way. He remembered seeing her years ago when, on a business trip to London, he had called briefly at Antonio's apartment to check in on his little brother. She had been a plump, plain-faced little schoolgirl in a baggy sweater, with long fair pigtails, who had been visiting her brother and was leaving as Lorenzo arrived. Her brother Damien had met Antonio at university in London, and they'd become firm friends and flatmates. A friendship that had ended tragically, and one he certainly did not need reminding of for a second time today...

'Sorry for the delay, but it was unavoidable.' She rose to her feet and he noted she had scarcely changed at all. Small—she barely reached his shoulder—with her hair scraped back in a knot on top of her head, her face free of make-up. The baggy sweater had been replaced with an equally voluminous black suit, with a long skirt that did her no favours at all. Slender ankles, he noted, and tiny feet, but the flat shoes she wore had definitely seen better days. She obviously cared little for her appearance—not a trait he admired in a woman.

Lucy Steadman looked up and up at the man standing in front of her. Antonio had told her once his brother was a lot older than him, and a staid, boring banker who did not know how to enjoy life, amongst other similarly harsh comments, and now she could see what he had meant...

Tall—well over six feet—he was dressed conservatively in a dark suit, a white shirt and plain dark tie. And expensively, she guessed. His broad shoulders were outlined superbly by the well-cut jacket, and she hastily lifted her gaze from where it had drifted down to his hips and thighs to fix on his face. The man was hard and unsmiling, but Antonio had missed one attribute that was immediately obvious to Lucy, even with her limited experience of men.

Lorenzo Zanelli was a truly arresting male, with a subtle aura of animal magnetism about him that any women past puberty could not fail to recognise. Given the severity of his clothes, surprisingly his thick black hair was longer than the current fashion and brushed the white collar of his shirt. The planes of his face were firmly etched , his heavy lidded eyes were brown, almost black, and deep-set beneath thick arched brows his nose large and definitely Roman and his mouth wide and tightly controlled.

'You must be Lorenzo Zanelli,' she said, and held out her hand.

'Correct, Miss Steadman,' he responded, and took her hand.

His clasp was firm and brief, but the sudden ripple of sensation that shot up the length of her arm affected Lucy well after he had dropped her hand, and she simply stared at him. She had the oddest notion he was familiar to her, yet she had no memory of ever having met him before, and he in no way resembled his brother.

He wasn't handsome in the conventional sense, but his face was fascinating. There was strength in his bold features—a powerful character that was undeniable—and the subtle hint of sensuality about his mouth intrigued her. Her gaze lingered on the perfectly chiselled lips, the bottom fuller than the top, and she found herself imagining what his kiss would taste like...sensuous and beguiling. A tiny shudder vibrated through her body and, shocked by her physical response to an uncharacteristic flight of fantasy, she swiftly raised her eyes and ignored her strange reaction to a man she had every reason to dislike.

Lucy excused her totally unprecedented lapse with the wry thought that Lorenzo Zanelli was the sort of man to make anyone look twice. In fact she would like to paint a portrait of him, she mused, slipping back in to her professional comfort zone.

'Miss Steadman, I know why you are here.'

His deep, slightly accented voice cut into her reverie, and she blinked just in time to see his dark eyes flick disdainfully over her. She felt the colour rise in her cheeks with embarrassment at having been caught staring. 'You do?' she murmured inanely. Of course he did—she had written to him...

Her original reason for this trip to Italy was to personally deliver a portrait she had painted of an Italian countess's recently departed husband. The lady had commissioned the painting after walking into Lucy's art and craft gallery with the friend she'd been visiting in England. Lucy had received via the post dozens of photographs of the man, and she had been thrilled that her work was finally going to get some recognition beyond the local scene.

Not that she was seeking fame—realistically, in today's world where a pickled sheep or an unmade-bed made millions—she knew she was never going to get it, but it was nice to feel appreciated for what she did excel at. She had a natural gift for catching the likeness and character of any subject, be it a stuffed dog—her first ever commission!—or a person. Her paintings in oils— full-figure or portrait, large canvas or miniature—were good, even if she did say so herself...

She had confirmed her trip to Verona with the Countess when she had finally managed to get an appointment with Signor Zanelli. After a phone call that had got her nowhere she had written to the Zanelli Bank, asking for its support in staving off the forced buy-out of Steadman Industrial Plastics by Richard Johnson, one of the largest shareholders in her family's firm. She had received a short letter back from some manager, stating that the bank did not discuss its policy on individual investments.

She had very reluctantly, as a last resort, written another letter and marked it 'Personal and Private', addressing it to Lorenzo Zanelli himself. From all she had heard about the man she had formed the opinion he was a typical super-rich alpha male, totally insensitive to other people and with the arrogant conviction that he was always right. He never changed his mind, not even when a formal inquest said otherwise, and she disliked him intensely…

Lorenzo Zanelli had been horrible to Damien after the inquest into the mountaineering accident that had caused Antonio's death, accosting him outside the courthouse and telling him coldly that while legally he might have been found innocent of any fault as far as he was concerned Damien was as guilty as hell, and might as well have cut Antonio's throat instead of the rope. Her brother, devastated by the loss of his friend, had felt badly enough as it was. Lorenzo Zanelli had made him feel a hundred times worse and he had never really recovered.

As far as Lucy was aware there had been no contact between the two families since, and it had come as a shock to her to discover after Damien's death the Zanelli bank was a third silent partner in her family firm. Lorenzo Zanelli was the last man she wanted to ask for a favour but she had no choice. Trying to be positive, she'd told herself maybe she was wrong about Lorenzo—maybe it had been his grief at losing his brother that had made him say horrible things to Damien, and with the passage of time he would have a much more balanced view.

So Lucy had swallowed her pride and written to him, blatantly mentioning her family's friendship with his brother Antonio. She had informed him she was visiting Verona for a day or two, and had almost begged for a few minutes of the man's time before finally being granted an appointment today.

The continuation of Steadman Industrial Plastics as a

family firm was dependent on Lucy persuading Zanelli to agree with her point of view. Not that she had any family left, but to the residents of the small town of Dessington in Norfolk, where she'd been born and had grown up, Steadman's was the main employer, and even though she had not lived there since graduating from college she did still visit occasionally, and she did have a social conscience—which she knew Richard Johnson did not.

She was pinning her hopes on Signor Zanelli. But now, after what she had heard about him and being faced with the man in person, she was having serious doubts.

She had arrived in Verona at ten this morning—well, not exactly *in* Verona. The budget airline she had travelled with had landed at an a airport almost two hours away. She'd just had time to book into her hotel and get here on time, and her flight back was tomorrow evening at eight. On her arrival at his office the great man's secretary had taken her name, made a phone call, and then told her in perfect English that Signor Zanelli was going to be delayed. She had asked her if she would like to reschedule the appointment and, flicking through a diary, had suggested three days' time.

Lucy had countered with a request for the next morning, sacrificing her plan to explore the town and the famed arena. Her appointment with the Contessa was in the afternoon. The secretary had told her it was not possible, but she could wait if she liked. She had had no choice but to agree.

'Miss Steadman?'

He repeated her name and, startled out of her wandering thoughts, she glanced up at him, green eyes clashing with brown. The arch look he gave her was all male arrogance.

'You're a determined little thing, I'll give you that,' he drawled and, turning to his secretary, said something in Italian that sounded like 'ten minutes—then call' before throwing over his shoulder, 'Come, Miss Steadman. This will not take much time.'

Lucy bit back the response that sprang to mind. It had already taken a heck of a lot of her time. Pausing for a moment, she tried to smooth the creased black linen skirt she wore—a pointless exercise—and watched the broad back of the man as he disappeared into his inner sanctum, the door swinging closed behind him. He might be strikingly attractive, but he was certainly no gentleman, and her nerves tightened a notch.

'You'd better go in now,' the secretary said. 'Signor Zanelli does not like to be kept waiting.'

Given how long *she* had been waiting—her appointment had been for two and it was now after three— Zanelli had some nerve, she thought, her temper rising. Dismissing the odd effect he had on her own nerve, she squared her shoulders and, taking a few deep breaths, walked across the room and into the man's office.

He was standing behind a large antique desk, talking rapidly into a telephone which he put down when he saw her.

'Take a seat.' He indicated a chair in front of the desk as he sank into a big black leather one behind it. 'Then say what you have to say, and make it quick—my time is valuable.'

He had not waited for her to sit down. In fact he was well on the way to being the rudest man she had ever met, and she had been right to dislike him sight unseen, Lucy decided, her green eyes sparking angrily.

She said without thinking, 'I can't believe you are Antonio's brother.'

Antonio had been handsome and lovable, and her brother Damien's best friend at university. Lucy had been fourteen when her brother had brought Antonio home the first time for the mid-term break, and she had developed a terrific crush on the young Italian—so besotted she had actually started taking Italian language lessons at school. Antonio, only four years older, but a decade older in experience, had not taken advantage— quite the opposite. He had treated her as a friend and had not made her feel foolish at all. Unlike this hard-faced man, looking at her across the wide expanse of the desk with cold eyes and without a tender bone in his body, she was sure.

'You are nothing like him. You *look* nothing like him.'

Lorenzo was surprised. Lucy Steadman had spirit. Her face had flushed with colour, highlighting the delicate bone structure. She wasn't plain as he had thought, but she *was* angry. His mouth tightened. He did not want to fight with her, he simply wanted her out of his sight as quickly as possible—before his anger got the better of him and he told her in return exactly what he thought of *her* brother...

'You are right. My younger brother was the beautiful one, both inside and out, whereas I—so Antonio used to tell me—am a serious, hard-headed banker with ice in his veins who should lighten up and enjoy life. Not that it did Antonio much good,' he said starkly.

For a moment Lucy thought she saw pain shadow his eyes as he spoke. She had been tactless, letting her dislike of the man show, and politely offered her sympathy. 'I am sorry...so sorry,' she murmured, as the memory of the tragic accident that had killed his brother and which she felt had been instrumental in the death of hers filled her mind. 'I understand how you feel,' she said, and began telling him about her brother.

'Damien never really got over losing his best friend.' She did not add *thanks in part to you,* but she thought it. 'He was never well afterwards. I was finishing my second year at college and tried to help, but it was no good in the end,' she admitted. 'Though he did begin working with my father in the business his heart wasn't in it. Then, when my father died the following year, it was another blow to him. With my father gone Damien could not manage everything, so he decided to hire a manager to oversee the running of the business and within a year everything seemed to be getting better. Then last year Damien went on holiday to Thailand and died there.' He had recklessly stopped taking his medication, and it still hurt Lucy to think of him. 'So I really do know how you feel.'

Lorenzo doubted that Lucy Steadman had an inkling of his real feelings, and he wasn't about to tell her. 'I'm sorry for your loss,' he said coolly. 'But now can we get down to business—the proposed sale of Steadman's, I believe?'

Lucy had almost forgotten the reason she was there as images of the past and this man filled her mind. Suddenly it hit her that she had not made a very good start, and the speech she had prepared had gone clean out of her head.

'Yes—no. Not a sale—I mean, let me explain...'

One devilish brow arched sardonically in her direction. 'I will give you five minutes,' he said, and looked pointedly at his wristwatch.

He had fine black hairs on his wrist, she noted, and

shook her head. What was she thinking…? *Concentrate,* she told herself.

'When my father died, in accordance with his will Damien inherited the family home in Dessington and seventy-five percent of the business. I had the other twenty-five and the holiday house in Cornwall. My father was not big on equality of the sexes.'

'I don't need your opinions—just facts.' Though he knew most of them. The manager in charge of the bank's small investments had kept him informed of any development at Steadman's over the years, but common courtesy decreed he listen to her. But now he realised the reason for the woman's unvarnished looks and clothes. Lorenzo was all for equality of the sexes, and made a point of employing and promoting intelligent women in his organisation, but he had no time for a latter-day women's libber who thought the world owed her a living without her having the requisite skills to earn one, and his patience was fast running out.

Lucy took a deep breath. 'After Damien died I inherited all that was left… Manufacturing plastics is not my thing, so I was quite happy to leave the running of the place to the manager while the lawyer dealt with probate. Unfortunately it was only when the lawyer finalised everything a couple of months ago, and called me in to explain my inheritance, that I discovered my father— with Damien's agreement—had seven years earlier made Antonio a partner in the business by selling him forty percent of the firm. I was still at boarding school at the time, and knew nothing about it, but apparently it was agreed between them all that Damien and Antonio were going to be partners in the business and run it between them when my father retired. Unfortunately Antonio died, so it was never to be.' She sighed, and then chewed nervously on her bottom lip. This was the hard part.

She raised a hand and counted off the fingers of the other hand to help her concentrate. 'So, after my father died I did not *actually* inherit twenty-five percent of the business.' She counted off a second finger. 'It was twenty-five percent of what was only sixty percent.' She counted a third finger. 'So that was twenty...no, wait... fift—'

'*Basta!* Enough.'

Lucy raised her head, her green eyes clashing with his 'You've put me off now,' she declared, waving her hands out wide.

'I'm a banker—I can do the maths. A word of advice—never go into business.' And she could have sworn she saw a hint of amusement in his dark eyes before the shutters came down and his hard, expressionless gaze fixed on her.

'Your time has run out, so I will put you out of your misery. Your brother—who was obviously quite keen on partners,' he said, with a hint of sarcasm in his tone, 'took on another partner eighteen months ago, selling fifteen percent of his share to Richard Johnson, who as it turns out is a property developer. Now your brother has died he wants to buy out the other two partners, demolish the factory and build a block of apartments on the land. You are six percent short of a majority on your own, and you want my bank, which now controls Antonio's investment, to side with you to stop the development.'

In that moment Lorenzo, who had been ambivalent over what action to take—a rare occurrence for him—made up his mind. He had toyed with the idea of supporting Miss Steadman—the monetary aspect was next to nothing to the bank, and it also meant he could avoid discussing with his mother a subject that would reignite the pain of her losing Antonio.

He was intensely protective of his mother—had been since his father's death, and even more so since the death of Antonio. She was a tender-hearted, compassionate woman, who had accepted the inquest result as gospel, and he had taken immense care to ensure she never found out about his confrontation outside the courthouse with Damien. He had paid off the reporter who had caught the declaration of his true view on the case.

But Lucy Steadman was not a good investment. She had been quite happy to let her father and brother keep her in comfort while spouting off about equality of the sexes, and frankly, after what he had learnt earlier today, any thought of assisting a Steadman in any way was anathema to him.

'Yes, that is exactly right—otherwise the factory will close and a lot of people will lose their jobs. That would be a devastating blow to Dessington, the town I grew up in, and I can't let that happen.'

'You have little choice. The factory just about breaks even, but makes very little profit for its partners and consequently is of no interest to this bank. We will be selling to Mr Johnson, who is offering a good return on our original investment.' He could not resist turning the screw a little. 'Bottom line—unless you can come up with a higher figure than that currently on offer to buy out my bank's interest in the next couple of weeks the sale will go through.'

'But I can't—I only have my shares.'

'And two houses, apparently. You could possibly raise money on those with your bank.'

'No—just one and a half. Damien mortgaged his,' Lucy murmured to herself. That was something else she had not known.

'Somehow that does not surprise me,' he drawled cynically and, rising to his feet, walked around the desk to stop in front of her. 'Take my advice, Miss Steadman, and sell out. As you said yourself, you have no interest in plastics, and neither does this bank.'

She glanced up the long, lithe length of him, her green eyes clashing with hard black.

'How old are you? Twenty—twenty-one?' he asked.

'Twenty-four,' she snapped. At five feet two and with youthful appearance, it had been the bane of her life at college, when she'd continually been asked for proof of her age. Even now she still had to carry identification if she wanted to enter licensed premises.

'Twenty-four is still young. Do as your brother did and have fun. Allow me to show you out.'

*Throw* her out, more like, Lucy thought, and panicked. 'Is that it?' She leapt to her feet and grasped his arm as he turned towards the door. 'No discussion? At the very least give me more time to try and raise the money. I'll do anything I can to save the factory.'

Lorenzo looked down into her eyes. They were an amazing green, he realised, big and pleading. He lost his train of thought for a moment...

He could do without Lucy Steadman and her persistence. He had known of her initial call to the bank, and that she had been sent the bank's standard response. When he'd received her personal letter informing him she was visiting Verona he had told his secretary to arrange a meeting for two reasons. Firstly out of respect for his mother's feelings, because she was the one who had given Antonio the money to buy his share in

Steadman's in the first place, without Lorenzo or the bank's knowledge, and it seemed she had a sentimental attachment to the investment.

It had only been after Antonio's death and the inquest, when Lorenzo had got around to dealing with his brother's personal estate, that he'd actually discovered his brother was a partner in Steadman's. He had queried his mother about the investment because the transaction had not been made through the Zanelli Bank but the Bank of Rome, and had suggested she sell. Her reply had astounded him.

Her own mother's advice when she'd married had been to always keep a separate account that one's husband knew nothing about, as it gave a wife a sense of independence. Obviously her account could not be at the Zanelli Bank, hence it was at the Bank of Rome. As for selling, she hadn't been sure—because it still gave her great comfort to know that Antonio had not been the lightweight people had thought, but had made plans for the future and intended being a successful businessman in his own right.

Lorenzo didn't agree. On finishing university Antonio and Damien had taken a gap year together, to travel around the world. That had spread into a second year, until their last mountaineering escapade that had seen Antonio dead at twenty-three. He doubted if either of them would have settled down to run a plastics factory... But he hadn't argued with his mother, and she had agreed to his suggestion that he buy the investment from her and bring it under the control of the Zanelli Bank.

The other reason he had agreed to meet Lucy Steadman was in memory of his brother. Because if he was honest he felt guilty. He had been so involved with work and his own business affairs that he had not paid as much attention to Antonio as he should have done. He had loved his brother from the moment he was born, but Antonio had been only eight when Lorenzo had left home for university, and holidays aside he had never returned, going straight to America after graduating. When he did return on the death of his father, to take over the bank, Antonio had been a happy-go-lucky teenager with his own group of friends. At eighteen he'd gone to live in London, so they'd never spent much time together as adults. But he remembered Antonio had mentioned Lucy a few times and had thought her a delightful child. So, although he despised her brother, he had agreed to see her. But after what he had learned over lunch today any fleeting compassion for a member of the Steadman family was non-existent.

Suddenly the frustration that had simmered inside him since speaking with Manuel exploded inside him, and the woman hanging on to his arm was the last straw. Abruptly he hauled her against him, covered her softly pleading lips, and kissed her with all the angry frustrated feelings riding him.

Lucy did not know what had hit her. Suddenly she was held against a hard body, and his mouth slammed down on hers. For a moment she froze in shock. Then she became aware of the movement of his firm lips, the subtle male scent of him, and excitement sizzled though her heating her blood and melting her bones. She had been kissed before, but never like this. He fascinated, thrilled and overwhelmed her every sense. When he abruptly thrust her away she was stunned by the immediacy of her response, and stood in a daze simply staring at him.

Lorenzo never lost control and was shocked by what

he had done—even more shocked by the sudden tightening in his groin. He looked down at the poorly dressed girl gazing at him and noticed the telltale darkening of the pupils in her big green eyes, the flush in her cheeks, the pulse that beat frantically in her throat. He realised she was his for the taking. He also realised he had definitely been too long without a woman to actually consider seducing this one.

'No, there is nothing you can do to make me change my mind. You are not my type,' he said, more harshly than was warranted.

Lucy blinked, snapping out of the sexual fog that held her immobile, and really looked at him. She saw the hard, cynical smile and realised he had actually thought she was offering him her body. Having kissed her, he wasn't impressed, and humiliation laced with a rising anger flooded through her.

'To be brutally frank, Miss Steadman, neither I nor the bank have any wish to continue doing business with a Steadman. You have wasted your time coming to Verona and I suggest you take the next flight out. Is that clear enough for you?'

Lucy saw the determination in his cold black eyes and knew he meant every word. She had the fleeting notion this was personal, and yet he didn't know her. But then again she'd disliked him without knowing him. Antonio had told her his brother was known as a brilliant financier and ruthless at negotiating with a hint of pride in his tone.

He'd been absolutely right, but she doubted he would have been proud of his brother had he lived to see this day. Antonio had been a gentle soul, whereas the man before her did not have one...

'Perfectly,' she said flatly.

Lucy was an artist, but she was also a realist. Her mother had died when she was twelve, and her father had never recovered from the loss of the love of his life. And then her brother last November. Lucy had learnt the hard way there was no point fighting against fate.

She stepped back, straightened her shoulders and, willing her legs to support her, walked past Lorenzo to the door and opened it. She turned and let her gaze sweep over him from head to toe. Big, dark and as immovable as a rock, she thought, and had to accept that short of a miracle she had little to no chance of saving Steadman Industrial Plastics.

'I can't say it was a pleasure meeting you, but just so you know I am in town for another day. You never know—you might change your mind.' She said it simply to goad the man—he was such a superior devil he needed someone to deflate his ego.

'Not this particular part of town. Security will have strict instructions not to allow you access. I want nothing to do with your business or you. Plump, brainless, badly dressed and mousy women have no appeal to me.'

'You really are the arrogant, opinionated, ruthless bastard Antonio said you were.' She shook her head in disgust, and left.

# CHAPTER TWO

SHOCKED rigid, Lorenzo stood for a moment, her words ringing in his ears. Her last comment had hit a nerve. Was that what Antonio had really thought of him? Not that it mattered now his brother was dead, but it was the way he had died that still rankled, and the photographs given to him today had not helped.

At the inquest Damien Steadman had been called to give evidence, along with the rescue service personnel who had found Antonio's body too late to save him. Damien had been the lead climber, and had reached the top of a forty-foot cliff-face when Antonio had lost his footing and been left suspended in mid-air. Damien had tried to pull him up, but had finally cut the rope binding them together, letting Antonio fall.

A few years earlier, after a television documentary about a similar incident where both men had ultimately survived, the mountaineering community had concluded cutting the rope was the correct action to take, as it enabled the lead climber to try and seek help for his companion. The same conclusion had been reached at Antonio's inquest. Damien Steadman had been exonerated of any fault—which had enraged Lorenzo. His mother, devastated by grief, had been too ill to attend, but he had sat through the entire proceedings and not been impressed by Damien's vague account. When Damien had had the nerve to approach him after the inquest, to offer his sympathy on the death of his brother, Lorenzo had lost it. He had told the young man as far as he was concerned he was as guilty as hell, he hoped he rotted in hell, and a lot more besides before walking away.

Five years later, with the grief and rage dimmed, he could look at the tragedy with some perspective, but it still did not sit easy with Lorenzo. He doubted he would have cut a rope on his friend, but then he had never been in that position—and Damien Steadman *had* eventually raised the alarm.

It was the *eventually* that disturbed him more now— that and the lingering taste of Lucy Steadman's lush mouth beneath his. Where the hell had *that* thought come from? he wondered. She was far too young, never mind the rest of her faults.

His decision to sell the Steadman's shares was the right one. His last connection to the Steadman family would be finally cut. He'd explain it to his mother somehow, and thankfully would never see Lucy Steadman again.

Banishing her from his mind, he sat down at his desk, clicked on the computer and called his secretary.

The following afternoon, after a restless night in the strange hotel bed, during which a large dark man who looked suspiciously like Lorenzo Zanelli had seemed to slip in and out of her dreams with a surprisingly erotic frequency, and a morning spent exploring Verona, Lucy exited the taxi outside a magnificent old building, feeling excited, if a little hot. But then almost every building in Verona was fabulous and old, she thought wryly.

She carefully placed her leather satchel holding the portrait on the desk in the foyer of the most luxurious apartment building in the city, according to the taxi driver who had brought her here. Looking around, she believed him as she handed her passport to the concierge at his request for identification.

She reached a hand around to rub her lower back. Carrying the satchel around all morning had not been a great idea, but she had not wanted to waste time returning to the hotel.

'The Contessa della Scala is at home, *signorina*. Number three—the third floor. But first I must call and tell her you have arrived.' He handed her passport back and, placing it back in her satchel, she glanced around the elegant foyer towards the elevator.

The doors opened and a man walked out—and her mouth fell open in shock as what felt like a hundred butterflies took flight in her stomach.

Dark eyes clashed with green. 'You!' he exclaimed, and in two lithe strides Lorenzo Zanelli was at her side. 'What do you think you are doing, following me around?' he demanded and grabbed her arm.

'Following you around? You must be joking,' Lucy jeered, the butterflies dying a sudden death at his arrogant assumption. She tried to shake off his hand, but with no luck. 'Oh, for heaven's sake, get over yourself and let go of me.'

'How did you get in here? This is a secure building.'

'Through the door. How do you think?' she snapped.

'And that is the way you are going out, right now—after I have had words with the incompetent concierge who allowed you to enter.'

At that moment the concierge put down the telephone

and turned back to smile at Lucy. But before he could speak Lorenzo Zanelli launched a torrent of Italian at the poor man.

Lucy's Italian lessons had not been completely wasted, but she could only understand Italian rather than speak the language, so she didn't try now. She watched with interest as Lorenzo's voice slowly faded as the concierge responded. She noted the slow dark flush crawl up the tanned olive-toned face and almost laughed out loud. The superior devil was totally embarrassed, and suddenly she was free.

Lorenzo Zanelli looked down at Lucy and saw the amusement in her green eyes, and for the first time since he was a teenager he felt like a prize idiot. What on earth had possessed him to think she was following him? Probably the same irrational urge that had made him kiss her yesterday. He was acting totally out of character—usually he was the most controlled of men—and it had to stop. But she *had* told him she was going to be in town another day and suggested he might change his mind, so his assumption was not that ridiculous. Obviously he realised she had been winding him up, but however he tried to justify his behaviour he still felt like a fool.

'I owe you an apology, Miss Steadman,' he admitted curtly. 'I am sorry; it seems you have every right to be here.'

'Apology accepted—but I bet it nearly choked you,' Lucy prompted with an irrepressible grin. There was something very satisfying in seeing the stiff-necked arrogant banker made to look a fool.

'Not quite, but close,' he said, his lips quirking at the corners in a self deprecating smile. 'So how do you know the Countess della Scala?' he asked.

His smile—the first she had seen from him—made her heart turn over. But, remembering their last meeting and what he was really like, she stiffened. 'Mind your own business,' she said bluntly. 'As I recall you told me quite succinctly yesterday you wanted nothing to do with mine.' And, brushing past him, she walked to the elevator and stepped inside.

The petite, elegant Countess was an absolute delight, Lucy thought ten minutes later, sitting in a comfortable chair and watching the elderly lady reclining on a sofa and examining the eighteen-by-twelve portrait of her husband that her manservant held a few feet away from her.

'I love it—absolutely love it,' she said, then instructed the manservant to place it on the table while she decided where to hang it. She turned back to Lucy. 'You have captured my beloved husband perfectly. All my friends will be green with envy, and I can see a lot more commissions coming your way and a great future ahead of you.'

'I hope so.' Lucy grinned. 'But thank you. I'm glad you like it, because it was a real pleasure to do—he was a very handsome man.'

'Oh, he was—and so jolly. Nothing like Lorenzo Zanelli. The nerve of the man, trying to have you thrown out of the building. Are you sure you are all right.'

'How on earth did you know about that?' Lucy asked in surprise.

'The concierge is a good friend of mine and keeps me informed of everything. Zanelli's behaviour was disgraceful—I can't imagine what he was thinking.'

'I had a brief meeting with him yesterday over something his bank has an interest in, and he jumped to the conclusion I was following him,' Lucy said with a grin. 'He obviously has an overblown sense of his attraction to women, or he is just paranoid. I had no idea he lived here.'

'Ah, my dear—Lorenzo Zanelli doesn't live here, but friends of his, Fedrico and Olivia Paglia, have an apartment here. Unfortunately Federico was injured in a hunting accident in January and has been in a rehabilitation clinic ever since. There has been the occasional rumour circulating about Lorenzo Zanelli's involvement with the poor man's wife, because he has visited Olivia a few times, though I can't see it myself. He is much more likely to be taking care of her husband's business affairs than *her*.' She chuckled. 'Zanelli has the reputation of being a loner, a very private man and a workaholic. Olivia Paglia is a real social butterfly—which is why I can't see the two of them together. They are like chalk and cheese.'

'They say opposites attract,' Lucy inserted, fascinated by the Contessa's conversation.

'Personally I don't believe it. But enough gossip. When we first met I was struck by how bright you looked, wearing a brilliant blue top and white tailored trousers. Now, I hope you won't take this the wrong way, my dear, but that black suit is ill fitting and absolutely dreadful.'

Lucy burst out laughing. 'I know—it's terrible. I borrowed it from a friend because turning up in jeans and a top or a colourful kaftan, which is pretty much all I own, didn't seem very businesslike. Plus, even though I had the portrait packaged I did not want to put it in the cargo hold. It took up most of my hand luggage, and I just managed to squeeze in a spare blouse and underwear.'

An hour later, against all her attempts to refuse, Lucy left with a vintage designer dress courtesy of the Contessa, and shoes to match.

She boarded the plane back to England with a spring in her step. She might not be able to save the family firm, but at least she had a nice cheque in her purse that would help, and a dress to wear for her friend Samantha's hen party this weekend. The following weekend was the wedding, and Lucy was to be the chief and only bridesmaid.

Lorenzo Zanelli viewed the procession down the aisle through cynical eyes. The bride, tall and attractive, looked virginal in white, with the extravagantly layered skirt of her gown cleverly concealing the fact she was pregnant. Another good man bites the dust! he thought, and wondered how James, an international lawyer and partner in his father's London law firm, had allowed himself to be caught so easily.

He had known James for years. His father was English and his mother Italian—her family home was on the shores of Lake Garda, near the Zanelli family home. He had met James as a teenager in the summer holidays at a local sailing club, and they had been friends ever since.

Usually Lorenzo avoided weddings like the plague, but now he was grateful he had accepted James's invitation—it could not have come at a better time. The past two weeks had seen his perfectly contented and well-ordered life severely disrupted.

First the photographs from Manuel had disturbed him so much he'd been angry on meeting Lucy Steadman, and behaved with less than his usual iron control. And then her expectation that he would agree to help her keep a business she had no interest in and that made little money had infuriated him still further. Kissing her had been a bad mistake, but how like a woman to expect a man to bail her out...

Then there was the complete and utter fool he had made of himself the next day. Instantly assuming the green-eyed little witch was following him. He still could not believe he had actually tried to have her thrown out of the building. For some reason her laughing eyes had featured in his dreams ever since, and why a plump little woman dressed not much better than a bag lady was disturbing his sleep he had no idea.

Maybe he was having a midlife crisis... His usual taste in women veered towards tall elegant brunettes, well groomed, immaculately dressed, and preferably with a brain...

The dinner party last Saturday with a few friends should have put him back on an even keel, but it had turned out to be a surprise birthday party arranged by Olivia Paglia—as if he needed reminding he was thirty-eight. His luck had continued its downward spiral when on Monday a photograph of him, with Olivia wrapped around him as they exited the supper club at two on Sunday morning, had appeared in the press, with an article full of innuendo.

The following day had brought a summons from his mother—the one woman in the world whose opinion actually mattered to him. His father had died when he was twenty-six, and he had been head of the family ever since—though he only occasionally stayed at the family home. He had various properties of his own that he used. Seeing the disappointment and anger in her eyes when she'd demanded an explanation for his behaviour with a married woman had bothered him.

Astonishingly, his mother had confided in him that she had always known her husband had kept a mistress. She had not liked it, but had accepted it. But even his father, for all his faults, would never have taken a married woman to his bed—and certainly not his best friend's wife...

Lorenzo could have told her his father had not had *one* mistress but two when he died. He knew because he had paid them off—plus he had known since he was a teenager of others, which had caused a rift between him and his father and was the reason he had gone to America to make his own way in the world. On his return he had discovered three more were on the books—his father had actually pensioned them off! Instead he'd bitten his tongue and listened as she berated him.

A Zanelli had never before been the subject of the tabloid press—he had disgraced the name. And then she'd got on to her favourite subject: it was past time he found a wife and settled down to produce a grandchild—an heir to the Zanelli name. Then, with tears in her eyes, she reminded him he was the only son left.

He had consoled himself that with luck, by the time he returned to Italy, the gossip started by the newspaper report would have blown over, and hopefully his mother would have forgotten as well. On flying into Exeter airport he had rented a car, and had driven down to Cornwall last night. He had booked into a country house hotel for the weekend, and would be flying out of London on Monday to New York for a week or two...

Much as he loved his own country, given the traditional position he had to uphold in Verona, he preferred the vitality of New York, where he usually had a lover. The women tended to be career-orientated, smart and sexy, and while his business affairs often appeared in the financial press his private affairs rarely registered on the press radar there. Whereas, given the status of the Zanelli name, in Verona, his every move was scrutinised by the gossip columns.

The bride passed by, and he caught sight of the single bridesmaid. For a moment he thought he was hallucinating.

Lucy Steadman... It couldn't be?

Her mousy hair was not mousy at all, but a kaleidoscope of colour, with hints of red and gold, swept up at the sides and held with a garland of rosebuds on the crown of her head, revealing her delicate features and then falling in soft silken waves down her back.

His dark eyes moved slowly in stunned amazement over her shapely body. The strapless sea-green dress she wore enhanced the creamy smoothness of her skin and clung lovingly to her full firm breasts, a handspan waist and slim hips. How had he ever imagined she was fat? he asked himself, and could not take his eyes off her.

She had the most supple, sexiest body he had ever seen, and he felt an instant stirring in his own as she glided down the aisle. The natural sway of her pert derrière forced him to adjust his pants. And this was the woman he had told he never wanted to see again...

Though on the plus side he suddenly realised his sexual antennae hadn't been at fault after all, but working perfectly when he had kissed her—which put paid to his mid-life crisis theory...

He had parted with his last lover Madeleine, a New York accountant, at New Year, because unfortunately she had begun to hint at commitment...something he was averse to.

But he definitely *did* need a woman—and a weekend affair with the luscious Lucy would suit him perfectly on so many levels. She lived in England—he divided his time mostly between Italy and New York. He could sate himself in her sexy little body with no danger of ever having to see her again. Unworthy of him, he knew, but he couldn't help thinking there would be a satisfying kind of justice in bedding Damien Steadman's sister and walking away...

Seated on the bride's side of the church, a misty-eyed Lucy watched as her friend Samantha and James Morgan, with eyes only for each other, took their wedding vows. No one could doubt the deep love they shared, and if ever a girl deserved happiness it was Sam, she thought.

Lucy had arrived at Samantha's parents' house, set on the cliffs above Looe, at eight that morning. They had all had breakfast together, and the rest of the time Lucy had spent in a kind of controlled chaos, getting dressed with the hairdresser and make-up artist fussing around her, while trying to keep Samantha calm and getting her ready for the service at two-thirty.

An hour ago Lucy had left for the church with the pageboy in a limousine, and—apart from having to take the little boy around the back of the old church for a pee—so far everything was going like a dream for her best friend.

Lucy had first met Samantha as a child, when she had spent every summer with her parents at their holiday home in Looe. They had both attended the children's Holiday Club and become friends. But after her mother died her father had refused to holiday in Cornwall any more, and consequently Lucy had lost touch with Samantha. It had only been after she had finished art college and inherited the family holiday home in Looe, setting up house and her own business there, that they had renewed their friendship.

Samantha had been one of the first customers in her art and craft gallery, and they had instantly recognised each other. They had both had troubled teen years— Lucy had lost both her parents, and Samantha had been diagnosed with leukaemia at the age of thirteen and fought a five-year-long battle to full recovery. Lucy knew that was the reason Samantha had got pregnant within two months of meeting James. Convinced her leukaemia treatment had left her infertile, she had never considered contraception necessary.

Lucy sighed. She was a romantic at heart. After all, Samantha had suffered before meeting James and falling in love. Getting married with a baby on the way was the perfect happy ending.

'Lucy, time to sign the register.' The best man, Tom, took her arm.

Ten minutes later the church bells began to peal, and the bride and groom walked back down the aisle as man and wife.

Lucy followed behind with Tom. She had met him at the rehearsal on Thursday night—he was James's best friend and a banker in the City. But nothing like the hateful, hard-faced banker she had met in Verona: Lorenzo Zanelli. Tom was fun.

The ceremony over, feeling totally relaxed, she glanced around the colourful congregation.

'You look beautiful, Lucy,' a deep, slightly accented voice drawled, and she almost dropped her posy of roses at the sight of the man sitting in the pew, his dark head tilted back, watching her.

She looked down into a pair of mocking eyes, her

mouth hanging open in shock. 'What are you doing here?'

'I was invited.'

'Move, Lucy—we are holding up the traffic.' She shut her mouth and was grateful for Tom's hand at her back, urging her on down the aisle.

Lorenzo Zanelli at Samantha's wedding—it wasn't possible.

Unfortunately it was, she realised as she spent the next half-hour at the bidding of the photographer as the wedding photos were taken. Somehow every time she looked up Zanelli seemed to be in her line of vision. Not surprising, she told herself. At over six feet, with broad shoulders and bold features, he had a presence about him that made him stand out in any crowd, and the superbly tailored silver-grey suit he wore with easy elegance simply enhanced his magnificent physique.

Seated at the top table at the wedding reception, Lucy tried to dismiss Zanelli's presence from her mind and give all her attention to Tom. He was easy to talk to, and when the meal was over and the speeches began his was one of the best.

The bride and groom opened the dancing, and then everyone else joined in. Tom turned out to be a good dancer and he made her laugh. When the music ended he led her to the side of the dance floor and said, 'Do you mind if I rescue my girlfriend now? She's bound to be feeling lonely, seated with strangers. I'll take you back to the table first.'

'Not necessary.' She smiled. 'I am going to find the powder room.'

'Okay!'

But Tom had barely been gone two seconds before Lorenzo Zanelli appeared at her side.

'Lucy, this *is* a pleasant surprise—can I have this dance?'

She tilted her head back to look a long way up into his harshly attractive face. 'I seem to recall you never wanted to see me again,' she said bluntly. 'So why bother?'

'Ah! Because I have never really seen you until now...' He stepped back and deliberately let his dark gaze roam over her, from head to toe and back up, to linger for a moment on the soft curve of her breasts revealed by the strapless dress, before his dark eyes lifted to capture hers with an unmistakable sensual gleam in their black depths.

Lucy fought down the blush that rose up her throat, but she could do nothing about the sudden hardening of her nipples against the soft silk of her gown.

'What is your English saying, Lucy? To hide one's light under a bushel?' His deep, melodious voice made his accent more pronounced. 'I never knew what a bushel was, but now thanks to you I do—a big, black shapeless garment.' One black brow rose enquiringly. 'I am right, yes?'

'No.' But she could not help her lips twitching. Even the Contessa had remarked on the ill-fitting suit.

'So I ask again—dance with me?' And before she knew it he had caught her hand in his.

The same tingling feeling affected her arm, and she burst into speech. 'How do you know James Morgan?' she demanded, slightly breathless, Lorenzo was not as staid as she had thought—he could turn on the charm like a tap—but she did not want to dance with him. She didn't like the man, and he had made it plain what he thought of her: nothing... But her own innate honesty forced her to admit she didn't trust herself up close to him. Tentatively she tried to ease her hand from his, but with no success. His long fingers tightened around hers.

'His mother is Italian and her parents' home is on the shores of Lake Garda. James and I met as teenagers when he visited with his family in the summer, and now whenever I need an international lawyer James is the man I call.' Reaching out, he slid his arm around her waist and drew her towards him.

Suddenly Lucy was aware of the warmth of his long body, the slight scent of his cologne, the masculine strength of him, in a purely carnal way that stunned her. She could not tear her eyes away from the mobile mouth, suddenly recalling the heart-stopping feel of lips that had once kissed hers as he continued speaking.

'I've never actually met the bride before, but that is not surprising. James has only known her eight months, and it is out of necessity a bit of a rushed affair, I believe?'

Charming, but definitely arrogant and opinionated, Lucy thought, no longer having any trouble raising her fascinated gaze from his mouth to look up into his dark eyes. Her own sparked with anger at his slur on Samantha.

'That is an unkind comment to make on what is a very happy day. Samantha is my friend, and for your information I happen to know it was love at first sight for both of them. Plus, James asked her to marry him *before* she knew she was pregnant.'

'You are a loyal little thing—and, I think, a hopeless romantic. But I bow to your superior knowledge and apologise for my thoughtless comment. Now, let's dance,' he ended with a grin.

His rueful grin and the proximity of his big body

were having a disastrous effect on her thought process. Biting back the yes that sprang to her lips, she stiffened in his hold. 'Why would I want to dance with a man who has sold my family business out from under me?'

The only place Lorenzo wanted the delectable Lucy was under *him,* and he saw his opportunity. 'There you are mistaken. The deadline is next week and I have not given the final go-ahead yet. It has occurred to me that if the land is valuable in the middle of a recession it will be a lot more valuable in the future.'

Lucy's eyes widened in surprise on his hard attractive face. Had he just said what she thought he had? 'You mean you are actually reconsidering your decision?' He lifted her hand and placed it against his chest, and she was instantly aware of the beat of his heart beneath her palm. Her own heart began to race. 'The factory could stay open for a while longer?' she prompted, a sudden huskiness affecting her vocal cords.

'It is a possibility to consider,' Lorenzo murmured, squeezing her hand and drawing her closer, well aware of how he affected her. 'But, as you said, this is a wedding and a happy occasion, so let us forget about business for now and enjoy the party.'

Against her better judgment, surprisingly Lucy did. Lorenzo was a superb dancer, she realised as they moved around the floor in perfect harmony. His hand on her back was firm and controlling, guiding her effortlessly to the music, and a long leg slid between hers as he spun her around. The only problem was her rapid pulse and the growing warmth spreading from her belly to every sensory nerve in her body. She glanced up at him, and her breath caught at the slumbering passion in the dark eyes that met hers.

She amended her earlier assessment. He certainly wasn't old. He was a superbly fit, incredibly attractive man, and her mouth went dry as another part of her anatomy shockingly did the opposite. Her lips parted slightly, the tip of her tongue circling them. She wasn't aware the music had stopped until Lorenzo briefly squeezed the hand he held against his chest and let it go.

He had damn near kissed Lucy on the dance floor, Lorenzo realised with a sense of shock, but she had given him plenty of provocation. Her sexy little body had moved against his with a sensuality that instantly aroused him. The scent of her, fresh and light, had filled his nostrils, and the soft silken smoothness of her skin beneath his palm, the gentle brush of her glorious hair against his hand on her back as they danced, had been a constant caress. Then she'd licked her lips, and he had been in imminent danger of embarrassing himself and her in front of everyone. He needed to get her alone...

Taking a step back, but keeping an arm lightly around her waist, he quipped, 'I think you deliberately hide your light under a bushel, Lucy—you have great rhythm.' And he was supremely confident he could induce her into being even more rhythmic in bed. Her fabulous body was made for sex. Looking down into the slightly dazed eyes of the woman curved in the crook of his arm, he added, 'But now I think a glass of champagne and some fresh air is needed.'

'Lorenzo?'

He heard his name called, but ignoring it, he attempted to steer Lucy away.

She looked over his shoulder. 'I think the man at the

table behind you is trying to get your attention...' she said, and he silently groaned.

'Come have a drink with us, Lorenzo!' the accented voice demanded.

# CHAPTER THREE

LORENZO recognised the voice, and good manners dictated it was a request he could not ignore. With his hand on Lucy's waist, he reluctantly turned.

A moment later Lucy, with Lorenzo's arm still around her waist and a glass of champagne in her hand, was being introduced to Aldo Lanza, the bridegroom's uncle from Italy, his wife Teresa, their two sons and their wives, and four grandchildren.

'Trust Lorenzo to grab the beautiful bridesmaid before anyone else had a chance,' Aldo said as he kissed Lucy's hand. Casting a knowing glance at the man holding her, he added, 'Don't be fooled by his easy charm—he can be a hard devil when you get to know him.' And he winked...

'I already gathered that,' Lucy said with a grin, enjoying Aldo's easy banter and putting her glass down on the table. 'We have met before.'

'Ah—you have visited Verona, perhaps? A beautiful city, no?'

'Yes, I have, and the architecture *is* stunning. The arena is amazing, too, but I did not have much time to look around as I was there on business.'

'Beautiful and clever. What line of business are you in?' he asked.

'Enough questions, Aldo,' Lorenzo interrupted. 'I'm sure Lucy does not want to discuss business at a wedding.' He had introduced Lucy without mentioning her surname, thinking the less Aldo knew the better—because his wife Teresa was the biggest gossip in Verona.

'No, really—I don't mind,' Lucy said swiftly. The arrogance of Lorenzo speaking on her behalf had touched a nerve. Her father and brother, much as she had loved them, had had a habit of doing the same. Which was partly the reason she had decided to move to Cornwall after her father's death, although Damien had been nothing but encouraging about her setting up her own business in Looe.

'I own an art and craft gallery here in the town. But I specialise in painting portraits, and was in Verona to deliver a completed commission to my client—a charming Italian lady. You may know her—the Contessa della Scala? In fact, I met Lorenzo in the foyer of her apartment block,' she said, giving Lorenzo a saccharine-sweet smile, reminding him he was not always as invincible as he thought...

Lorenzo's dark eyes narrowed angrily on her mocking green. It was the worst thing she could have said, given his recent appearance in the gossip columns. The Lanzas knew Olivia Paglia had an apartment in the same building.

Suddenly Lucy was aware of a pause in the conversation, and she wondered if she had gone too far. Then Aldo said something in Italian to his wife, and Teresa frowned. Looking at Lorenzo, she spoke equally swiftly.

Lucy looked on in amazement as the conversation became animated between the three, with much waving of hands. She barely caught a sentence, but was enthralled by Lorenzo's deep husky voice—and then she heard Aldo repeat the words 'Contessa della Scala' and all eyes turned on her.

'You know the Contessa della Scala well?' Teresa asked in English.

'I wouldn't say well, but I have met her couple of times and spoken to her on the phone. She is a lovely lady, and a delight to talk to.'

'Oh, so clever and *bella signorina*…' Teresa switched back into Italian, and the conversation went right over Lucy's head again.

Lorenzo's hand slowly tightened around Lucy's waist. He thought he had covered well by telling them they had met a couple of times and he had known Lucy for a while—which wasn't an outright lie. But then he'd had to field a dozen questions about his 'artist friend' and he'd realised he actually knew next to nothing about Lucy and had jumped to the assumption she did nothing. He also realised he had made an even bigger fool of himself than he had imagined, presuming Lucy had come to Verona specifically to see him about the Steadman deal when her main priority had obviously been her own business.

The chatter that had broken out at her comment and Lorenzo's fingers biting into her waist surprised Lucy. His dark head was bent towards her, and he spoke softly against her ear.

'You could have told me you are an artist, Lucy.'

His warm breath and the way he said her name did funny things to her tummy, and she wriggled out of his hold just as James appeared and saved her from answering.

'I see you have met the Italian side of my family,

Lucy—and now it is my turn to dance with the brides-maid, according to my wife Samantha.' He said *wife* with such pride Lucy smiled. And, glad of the reprieve from Lorenzo's constant presence, she let James lead her on to the floor.

'They can be a bit overwhelming *en masse,* and Sam thought you might need rescuing.'

'Not really—they all seem charming, if a little intimidating.'

She danced with James, and then threw herself into circulating and lost count of the number of men she danced with. With relief she accepted when Samantha asked her to accompany her back to the house and help her get changed into her honeymoon outfit. Her wedding dress, though fabulous, was killing her, she said, and as Lucy had stitched her into it in the first place, when a seam had split, she knew just what she meant.

Half an hour later she lined up with most of the guests along the drive as Samantha and James drove away in his treasured vintage green e-type Jaguar sports car.

Waving with one hand, Lucy wiped a few tears of joy for her friend from her cheek with the other.

'Proof positive of my suspicion that you are a hope-less romantic.' A long arm wrapped around her waist and she was spun round against a hard male body. 'Here—use this.' Lorenzo handed her a pristine white handkerchief.

'It's not necessary.' She placed her hands on his chest and pushed herself free of his hold. 'But thank you,' she said politely.

She had been carefully avoiding him for ages, and if their eyes had met accidentally she had quickly glanced away. But she hadn't been able to help noticing he'd had no shortage of dance partners all night. Not that she had been looking! And now he had caught up with her...

Lorenzo slipped the hanky in his jacket pocket and, taking her hand in his, said, 'Walk with me, Lucy. I don't feel like returning to the party just yet, and as Samantha's friend you must know these gardens well. You can lead me around.'

In more ways than one, Lorenzo acknowledged wryly. He couldn't remember the last time he had been so physically attracted to a woman he'd had to make a determined effort to prevent his body betraying him every time he looked at her.

Lucy was about to refuse when suddenly she remembered he had held out some hope for Steadman Industrial Plastics and agreed. Maybe she could talk to him sensibly and get him to agree to keep the factory open. The only slight problem with that idea was she simply had to look at Lorenzo for every sensible thought in her head to vanish. And the warmth of his hand holding hers seemed so right, so natural, she had no desire or will to break free.

They strolled down to where the garden ended at the cliff-edge, and looked out over the sea. The sun was just beginning to set over the far side of the bay.

'Do you realise the twenty-first of June is the longest and lightest day of the year in the northern hemisphere—the ideal day for a wedding? And at midnight there is going to be a magnificent fireworks display.' She was babbling, but Lorenzo made her nervous—and a lot of other things she wasn't ready to face just yet.

She didn't like the man. He was arrogant and rude, and a staid, boring banker was not high on her checklist of what she looked for in a man. Then again, she had never found *any* man who ticked her boxes... In fact after her one attempt at sex she had decided she was probably frigid and could happily stay celibate. But somehow Lorenzo Zanelli had the power to drive her senseless with only a kiss. She had dated a few men, but none had turned her legs to jelly the way Lorenzo did by simply holding her, and it frightened her.

'Why didn't you tell me you were an artist when we met?'

'You never asked.'

'I did ask why you were at the Contessa's—you could have told me then.'

'I could—but as you had just tried to have me thrown out of the building and called me a plump, brainless, badly dressed and mousy woman the day before, I didn't think you deserved an answer.'

'I'm sorry. I want to apologise for that day in my office. My comment was totally uncalled-for. I had a picture of you in my mind from the first time I saw you at my brother's apartment in London. You were a schoolgirl in a baggy sweater and pigtails, and I didn't really look past that.'

'I *thought* there was something familiar about you!' Lucy exclaimed, a long-forgotten memory surfacing of a big, dark frowning man in a dark suit once arriving at Antonio's apartment as she was leaving.

'Yes, well—now I know my view of you was totally false,' he said, with a self-derisory smile. 'But you caught me on a really bad day. My business lunch had gone on for far longer than it should have and I was badly delayed. I was running hopelessly late—unheard of for me. I'm not usually so...'

'Insufferably arrogant? Opinionated? Superior?' she offered cheekily. 'I may not be a whiz with numbers, like you, but when it comes to physical figures I am really good.'

One look at her walking down the aisle of the church had told Lorenzo *that,* but he bit back the sexual innuendo that sprang to mind. 'I really am sorry for my boorish behaviour.' He gently squeezed her hand. 'Please can we forget our first meeting and begin again?'

It was the *please* that did it. His apology sounded genuine, and Lucy glanced back up at him and was lost in the warmth of the sincerity in his deep brown eyes. 'Yes, okay,' she agreed, and suddenly shivered.

'Here—take my jacket,' Lorenzo offered, letting go of her hand to open his jacket.

'No, really—I'm fine.'

His lips twisted in a slow smile and, catching her hand again, lacing his fingers through hers, he cradled her hand on his chest. His other arm encircled her waist to pull her pliant body into the warmth of his. 'Then let me warm you...'

His dark head bent, and Lucy knew he was going to kiss her. When his lips brushed lightly against hers she felt her heart turn over. Never in her life had she experienced the dizzying sensations swirling around inside her that his kiss evoked. Her lips parted beneath his and the subtle invasion of his tongue into the moist heat of her mouth had her closing her eyes. Her free hand reached up to clasp his broad shoulders and cling as he folded her closer still. The blood bubbled in her veins and she was wildly, gloriously aware of sensations she had never experienced before. When she felt his hand stroking up her spine, finding her bare back under the tumbling mass of her hair, she trembled.

'Ah, Lucy!' He sighed, and broke the kiss, his dark eyes gleaming down into hers. He dropped soft kisses on her brow, her glowing cheeks, and then bent his dark head to say huskily against her ear, 'This is the time, but not the place. I think—'

Lucy never did hear what he thought, as they were once more interrupted by the booming voice of Aldo Lanza, calling out his name.

'I think I could kill that man,' Lorenzo ground out, but straightening up, held her lightly against his side as he responded.

The rest of the evening took on a dream-like quality. At Aldo's insistence they rejoined his party in the marquee. Lorenzo swirled her around the dance floor in his arms and she felt as if she was floating on air. Between dances he told her he had an apartment in Verona and one in New York, and he split his time between the two. His mother lived in the family home on Lake Garda, and he visited as often as work allowed. Apparently she suffered from angina and was quite frail. Lucy told him about art college in London and starting her business here in Looe, and how much she loved being her own boss.

For Lucy the night took on a magic all of its own as Lorenzo, holding her to his side, took her to gather with all the other guests in the garden to watch the fireworks display on the stroke of midnight.

How had she ever thought she disliked him without knowing him? So Lorenzo had lost his temper with Damien after the inquest? In fairness, it had to have been a traumatic time for him, and she could not really blame Lorenzo for Damien going off the rails afterwards. Lucy had sacrificed a lot for Damien, given him much more help than most sisters ever did, and yet his reckless behaviour had negated her help and ultimately led to his tragic death.

And how had she ever thought Lorenzo was boring? she wondered as he laughed and joked with the other guests as they said their goodbyes. She was totally captivated, her eyes shining like stars as she looked up at him as he turned back to her.

'The party is almost over, Lucy. Can I take you home now?' he asked, and the question in the glittering dark eyes said so much more.

'I am staying here tonight—to help with the clearing up,' she said reluctantly.

'Do you have to?' His long fingers curled about her wrist, his thumb carelessly caressing the soft underside, sending shivers of awareness through her body. 'I could tell our hostess you are too tired and I'm taking you home for some much needed rest.'

Her eyes locked with his, and the sexual tension that had sparked between them all evening heightened almost to breaking point. They both knew it was not a rest he was suggesting. Lucy's pounding heart wanted to say yes, but her head and her conscience was telling her to say no. She couldn't—she had promised. And then Samantha's mum interrupted them.

'There you are, Lucy. I was looking for you.'

Ten minutes later Lucy was seated in the passenger seat of Lorenzo's car on the way home, not sure how it had happened.

Lorenzo walked around the bonnet of the top-of-the-range BMW he'd rented and opened the passenger door. Reaching for her hand, he helped her out of the vehicle. He had sensed Lucy mentally pulling away from him as they had made the short journey to the outskirts of the town, and he needed to keep physical contact with her.

He wasn't about to strike out now. It had occurred

to him, as the evening wore on and he'd watched her dance, smile and flirt with a variety of men, that far from being too young and not possessing the traits he looked for in a lover—as he had thought when they'd met in Verona—the opposite was true. She was the perfect sexual partner for a weekend.

Lucy Steadman was no ordinary little small-town girl but an artist, accustomed to a bohemian lifestyle from her years at art college in London, and now living in Cornwall—the most popular county in England for artists and latter-day hippies. She was a free spirit and, judging by her response when he held and kissed her, and her body that oozed sex appeal, she had to be a woman well-versed in the pleasures of the flesh.

'Here—let me take the key.' He took the key she had taken from her purse and opened the door.

Lucy turned to close the door and found Lorenzo doing it for her. 'Would you like a coffee?' she asked, glancing up at him.

Slowly he shook his head and reached out one long finger, stroking her cheek in an intimate gesture.

'You know what I want—what we both want—and it isn't coffee,' he husked. 'I've been aching to do this again for hours.' And his arm wrapped around her waist, his mouth found hers, and she was lost in the wonder of his kiss.

Her mouth was warm and eager for his, and it never occurred to Lucy to resist. Her purse fell unnoticed to the floor as she reached for him, her hands clinging to his broad shoulders, her lips parting to the probing demand of his tongue, and she closed her eyes and gave herself up to the exciting sensations rioting around her body.

'The bedroom,' he groaned, and she indicated the

stairs with her hand. He swept her up in his arms and with unerring accuracy found her bedroom.

He lowered her down onto the white coverlet of the queen-sized bed and straightened up, swiftly shrugging off his jacket and removing something from the pocket. He dropped it on the side table as his jacket fell to the floor, followed by the rest of his clothes.

Lucy's eyes widened in awe as, lit by the light of the moon shining through the window, she saw his magnificent body naked.

She had seen naked men before, in life class at college, but the models had been mostly grey-haired elderly men, carefully posed. And she had made love once with a boy—Philip, who had shared an apartment with her and two other girls at college. It had been the same night that she'd seen a newsflash on the television about two climbers in an accident on Mont Blanc, giving Damien and Antonio's names. One had been thought seriously injured but it hadn't been stipulated which. She had been terrified for both of them. Philip had tried to find out more, without any success, and then taken her in his arms to soothe her fears. They had ended up making love. With hindsight it had been comfort sex, with both of them half clothed and he as inexperienced as her. She had been thoroughly ashamed afterwards, and wary of men ever since.

But nothing had prepared her for Lorenzo, standing boldly in the flesh... She could not take her eyes off him. His shoulders were wide, his chest broad, with a shadow of black body hair that tapered down to a narrow waist, flat stomach, lean hips and long legs. He was also mightily aroused, and she swallowed hard suddenly, slightly afraid.

'Are you waiting for me to undress you or admiring

the view?' he asked, with the confident grin of a man totally at ease in his naked masculinity. Not waiting for an answer, he knelt on the bed and pressed fervent little kisses on her face, her throat, while his hands, with a deftness she could only wonder at, removed her dress.

Beneath, she was wearing only white lace briefs, and a thousand nerve-endings sprang to life as he hooked his fingers in the lace and slowly pulled them down her legs.

'You are beautiful—so beautiful, Lucy.' He dropped a kiss on her stomach and she trembled in helpless response as his hands palmed her breasts, his thumbs gently grazing the burgeoning nipples, bringing them to rigid points of aching pleasure.

Lucy's response was a low moan as quivering arrows of sensation shot from her breasts to her pelvis.

'Perfect,' he murmured, and his mouth closed over a pert nipple, his tongue licking and suckling.

Her back arched involuntarily, and little whimpering sounds of pleasure escaped her as with frightening expertise Lorenzo delivered the same erotic torment to the other breast, before he found her mouth again and kissed her long and deep as his hands caressed her skin, shaping her waist, her hips, her thighs...

She reached for him, her small hands clasping his shoulders, stroking around her neck, holding him closer, her fingers raking through the thick black hair of his head, desperate for more.

Suddenly he reared back. 'I want you, Lucy. *Dio,* how I want you.' He groaned and nudged her legs apart, to settle between her thighs, and she could feel the hard pressure of his erection against her pelvis as he pinned her to the bed, kissing her with a deep, demanding passion that aroused an answering passion in her—a need, a longing that banished any faint doubt from her mind.

The rough hair of his chest rubbed against her swollen breasts, and her body felt electrified by the heat, the power of him. He kissed her throat, her shoulders, his mouth hard, and one hand curved under her hips to lift her slightly.

His mouth found the rigid tips of her breasts again, suckling first one and then the other, while his other hand dipped between her thighs, his long fingers exploring the hot moist centre of her with devastating skill.

She writhed achingly beneath him, her nails digging into the satin-smooth skin of his shoulders. She was white-hot with wanting, her need for him shuddering through her, the emotion so intense it was almost pain.

He lifted her hips higher, her legs involuntarily parted wider—and he was there, where she ached for him. She groaned as she felt him ease into her. There was the slightest twinge of pain as her moist sheath stretched to accommodate him, then exquisite hot, pulsating power as Lorenzo thrust slowly deeper and then withdrew.

Her body screamed with tension and she locked her legs around him, frantic for him to continue. He thrust again, deeper and faster, possessing her completely, and she cried out as her body convulsed in a million explosive sensations so intense her breath actually stopped with the sheer ecstasy of it all. She was aware of one last mighty thrust as her internal muscles still convulsed around him, and gloried in the great shudders that racked Lorenzo's huge frame. She was filled with a sense of oneness, a completion she had never imagined existed.

Lorenzo rolled off Lucy, his breathing ragged, his

heart pounding and his head spinning. She was everything he had expected and much more. She was so responsive... He couldn't remember losing control so completely ever before in his life. Of course he *had* been without a woman for a while, he rationalised, and, turning, he looped an arm around her shoulders and tucked her pliant body against his side.

'Are you okay? I didn't hurt you?' he asked. She was so small, so tight, that for a fleeting moment he had wondered if she was a virgin, but had quickly dismissed the thought. Lucy was obviously a woman of the world.

'No—quite the reverse,' she murmured softly, in a voice full of emotion at the wonder of him. She laid her hand on his broad chest. 'I am better than okay—sublime.' Rising up on one elbow, she leant over him and pressed a kiss on his chin—the highest she could reach. 'You, Lorenzo, are nothing like the staid banker I thought.' She looked up at him, her green eyes dazed with love, and gave him a languorous smile. 'You're brilliant, the most perfect lover in the...' She was about to say *world*, but a wide yawn stopped her.

'Glad to be of service,' he said softly. Running his hand through the tumbled mass of her hair, he smoothed it from her face and dropped a gentle kiss on her brow before folding his arms around her.

Lucy buried her head on his chest and, safe in the cradle of his arm, fell asleep.

Lucy slowly opened her eyes and blinked as the early-morning rays of the sun shining through the window dazzled her. For a moment she was disorientated and, yawning, stretched her slender body. She felt aches in places she had never felt before and, dreamlike, the events of the night fluttered through her mind.

She glanced across the bed and saw the indentation in the pillow and realised it wasn't a dream but reality. She had made love with Lorenzo Zanelli not once but twice... The first time had been incredible, and she'd thought nothing in the world could be better, but Lorenzo had proved her mistaken.

She had fallen asleep, exhausted, and it might have been minutes or an hour later when she'd awoke to find the bedside light on—just as a naked Lorenzo had strolled out of her *en suite* bathroom. What had followed had been a revelation in eroticism.

With a skill and an expertise she could only marvel at he had kissed and caressed her, encouraging her to do the same to him, and she had in the process discovered a sensual side of her nature she had never known she possessed. Finally Lorenzo had made long, slow love to her, almost driving her out of her mind as he'd taken her to the brink of paradise over and over again, until in the end she'd been begging for the release that only he could give her.

She looked around the room. No sign of his clothes— he was gone...

She closed her eyes and groaned, blushing at the thought of how wantonly she had behaved. Lorenzo probably thought she behaved that way with any man and considered her nothing more than a one-night stand. Mortified, she pulled the coverlet up over her naked body.

'A little late for modesty,' a deep, dark voice drawled, and she opened her eyes to see Lorenzo walking towards her.

'I thought you had gone,' she blurted, pulling herself up into a sitting position and tucking the coverlet under her arms while her eyes drank in the sight of him. He was dressed in the same grey suit, slightly crumpled now, and his white shirt was open at the neck, revealing the slightest glimpse of his dark chest hair. In his hand he held a mug of coffee.

'As if I would, after what we shared and I hope we can share again,' he prompted and, crossing to the side of the bed, deposited the mug of coffee on the bedside table. 'For you—I thought you might need the caffeine.' And he gave her a wicked smile that made her blush.

'Thank you,' she said, and picked up the mug and took a long drink of coffee. Lorenzo hadn't walked out on her, and he obviously did *not* think of her as a one-night stand. He wanted to see her again—he had said so—and his words warmed her heart and squashed all her doubts. 'You are right—I did need that.' She grinned up at him. 'But you should have woken me. You're the guest—I should have made it for you.'

He sat down on the bed and, leaning forward, lightly brushed her lips with his. 'No, it was my pleasure, Lucy. You are one very sexy lady. And you had a long day yesterday and an even longer night.'

His dark gaze met hers and she could not look away. The latent sensuality in his eyes was mesmerising her. A heated blush coloured her cheeks, and other parts of her were equally warm. 'Even so…'

'No, don't argue. I thought you needed to sleep, but then I remembered you told me Sunday was one of your busiest days in the tourist season, and you open at ten. So I decided to leave before anyone turns up.'

'What time is it?' Lucy demanded, panicking. Her head had cleared of the sensual haze Lorenzo's presence seemed to cause.

'Nine—you have plenty of time.' And, standing up, he looked down at her, his expression suddenly serious.

'I hope you don't mind but I had a look around. It is a nice place you have here—living accommodation upstairs and the gallery on the ground floor. But I couldn't help noticing you only have one lock on the front door. Your security is very poor—especially for a woman living on her own.'

Lucy drained her mug of coffee and placed it on the table. There was nothing wrong with her security, but she was thrilled by the thought that he was concerned for her safety. It had to mean he cared. She glanced up at him, her eyes sparkling with humour. 'Lorenzo, you are beginning to sound like a stuffy banker again.'

'If we had time I would show you I am not.' He chuckled, and reached down to clasp her head between his strong hands and kiss her senseless. 'Unfortunately we don't have time.' He straightened up. 'But I'll come back this evening and take you out to dinner. What time do you close?'

Breathless, Lucy said, 'I close at four—but if we are going out...'

'I'll see you at seven,' he husked and, planting a swift kiss on her head, he left.

Lucy watched him leave with a beaming smile on her face. Lorenzo didn't just want sex. He was actually taking her on a date. That had to be a good sign...

# CHAPTER FOUR

THE doorbell rang, and Lucy, with one last glance at her reflection in the mirror, adjusted the spaghetti straps of the bright blue summer dress she wore, picked up her purse and ran downstairs to open the door.

'You look fabulous,' Lorenzo said, and Lucy simply looked.

She had never seen him wear anything but a perfectly tailored suit—the uniform of choice for a seriously powerful conservative male. But now, casually dressed in pale trousers and a white shirt, with a cashmere sweater draped across his wide shoulders, his black hair dishevelled by the breeze and with a smile of wickedly masculine appreciation curving his lips, he could have been a latter-day pirate. She tilted back her head to look into his eyes and saw banked-down desire in the dark depths. Her own widened in instant response.

'Don't look at me like that, Lucy, or we will never get to dinner,' he said ruefully and, slipping an arm around her waist, he lowered his mouth down to hers as though he could not help himself.

At the first gentle brush of his lips Lucy's parted eagerly beneath his and she melted against him, her knees going weak as he kissed her with a subtle promise of passion.

'We have to go now,' he said huskily, and, keeping a hand on her back, took her key and urged her out of the house, locking the door behind them.

Right at that moment Lucy realised she would quite happily go to the end of the earth with Lorenzo, and suddenly the confusion, the butterflies in her stomach whenever she saw him, and the incredible joy she had felt when they made love all made sense. For the first time in her adult life she was experiencing the magic of overwhelming sexual attraction to a man. She had only ever read about it before, and never been able even to imagine it, but now she could—and maybe more!

Later, sitting opposite him at the table in dining room of the country house hotel where he was staying, she fell even deeper under his spell if that was possible.

Over the meal, with some prompting from him, she told him more about her business and the three fellow artists who displayed their wares in her gallery. Leon was a brilliant woodcarver, Sid was a potter, and his wife Elaine—who worked in the gallery on a permanent basis—had a talent for tapestry and quilting. She was also the owner of the big black linen suit...

Lorenzo seemed impressed, and told her a little more about himself. He was an amusing and informative conversationalist. She learnt he worked between Italy and New York and occasionally London, where the bank kept an office dedicated to the UK stock market. He owned a villa in Santa Margherita, and liked to spend his leisure time sailing his yacht around the Mediterranean.

'I'm sorry, Lucy, I must be boring you. Would you like to go on somewhere else? A club or casino maybe?' he said earnestly.

'You could never bore me, and I don't think there is either of those around here,' she informed him wryly.

And a casino wasn't exactly where she had imagined their evening would end.

A vivid image of his naked body gloriously entwined with her own made a blush rise up her throat, and she glanced across at him. He read her mind, and a knowing sensual smile curved his firm lips. Their eyes met, and the air between them was suddenly heavy with sexual tension.

'Let's get out of here.' Lorenzo abruptly stood up and, moving around the table, took her hand. He helped her to her feet and quickly out of the dining room, his hand gripping hers as he led her up the grand staircase to his first-floor suite.

She glanced around as he closed the door behind them. It was a sitting room with a fireplace—and she never saw the rest as Lorenzo swept her up in his arms...

Covering her mouth with his, kissing her with a hungry, driven passion, he carried her through to the bedroom. They fell on the bed in a tangle of arms and legs, mouths and hands. Lorenzo quickly divested her of the blue sundress she wore, and Lucy was no slouch in tearing at his shirt buttons. Within seconds they were both naked. There was no foreplay, just a frantic coupling, and they came together in an explosion of raw passion.

'I needed that,' Lorenzo groaned, and curved her into the hard heat of his body.

What followed was a lazy love-fest as he kissed her gently and explored every inch of her. Between talking nonsense and laughing, he trailed tender kisses down the length of her spine, asking about the scar he found there. Lucy chuckled, telling him it was just a cut, and then, turning, explored equally thoroughly down the front of *his* great torso. The end result was ecstasy...

'Wake up, Lucy.'

She opened her eyes and snuggled closer to his strong body. 'You are insatiable,' she murmured, wrapping her arm around his waist and lightly kissing his chest. They had made love twice already, but even so, pressed against him flesh on flesh, she felt the familiar quiver of desire snake through her body.

'Sorry, Lucy, I hate to disappoint you, but it really is time I took you home. I have to leave at dawn to drive to London—I'm flying out to New York about noon.' And, rolling off the bed, he shot her a brief smile and strolled across to the bathroom.

Lucy watched him go, admiring his bronzed body—the broad back, elegant spine, the firm buttocks and long legs—and feeling slightly disappointed. Silly, she knew, but she couldn't help wondering if this was it.

She slid out of bed and, gathering up her underwear and dress from the floor, slipped them on. Her sandals were by the door, where they had fallen along with her purse, and after slipping her feet into the high heels she straightened up. She caught sight of her face in the dresser mirror and almost groaned. No make-up, and her hair all over the place. Taking a comb from her purse, she mechanically ran it through her hair, sweeping the long mass behind her ears. She didn't want to think of Lorenzo's departure...

He reappeared from the bathroom, wearing boxer shorts, and as she watched he slipped on trousers and pulled a sweater over his head. Then, glancing at her, he quipped, 'You look ready for more...' with a devilishly suggestive arch of a black eyebrow. 'Come on—before I change my mind.'

Not sure if that was a compliment or not, she smiled and they left.

Sitting in the car five minutes later, as he drove in silence through the country lanes, Lucy cast him a side-long glance. She tried to tell herself she was worrying over nothing—Lorenzo was a busy man and of course he had to leave—it didn't mean she would not see him again. She looked at him. His attention was centred on the road ahead, his hands resting lightly on the steering wheel as he manoeuvred the car through the narrow roads with ease and speed. At this rate she would be home in a few minutes, she realised.

'So, when will I see you again?' she asked, and without thinking rested her hand on his leg.

Lorenzo tensed. Originally he'd had no intention of seeing Lucy again. But as he looked down at her hand, her small soft fingers, then lower to her shapely legs curved towards him, suddenly a picture of those same legs locked around him and her cries of pleasure as he thrust into her hot, tight little body filled his mind. Somehow the weekend affair he had planned didn't seem such a great idea after all...

He had been without a woman for months, he was a free agent, and the two nights he had spent with Lucy had been incredible. He could not remember ever having such great sex or such fun with a woman, and he was reluctant to give her up. In fact, he mused, keeping Lucy as a lover, quietly tucked away in a corner of England, held a lot of appeal. He visited London occasionally, usually flying in and out in a day, but that could be altered.

He decided to leave his options open.

'Soon, I hope. But, like you, I do have to work, I'll try and get back next weekend—if not the week after. But I'll give you a call.'

Lucy sighed with relief as Lorenzo stopped the car and after walking around the bonnet helped her out. The summer dress she wore was no protection against the cool night air and she shivered. Lorenzo looped an arm around her shoulders and walked her to the front door. Taking the key from her purse she looked up at him. 'Would you like to come in for a nightcap?' she asked hopefully, reluctant to see him go.

'I won't, if you don't mind,' he said with a rueful smile. 'Because if I do I'll kiss you, and it won't stop there.'

'No...I don't mind now I know you are coming back again,' Lucy responded blithely.

'Good.' Dropping a brief kiss on the top of her head— he didn't dare do anything more—he said, 'Now, lock the door behind you.'

Lorenzo's arm fell from her shoulders and she turned and put the key in the lock. Then she suddenly remembered why she had met him in the first place, and spun back.

'Wait a minute, Lorenzo—we never got around to discussing Steadman's, and we need to before Tuesday.' Then she remembered something else. 'You don't have my number. I'll give—'

'No need. The bank will have it,' Lorenzo stated.

Her words were a timely reminder. He had her number in more ways than one, he thought, his dark eyes narrowing cynically on her face. Her head was turned towards him, her green eyes incredibly large and luminous, the light of the moon making her pale skin almost translucent. Her long hair, swept back behind her small ears, seemed to fall in a shimmering mass down her back. Beautiful, and temptation personified, but not to him...not any more.

'Oh, yes—of course.' She turned completely around and smiled up at him. 'But about the factory...Tuesday is the deadline, and I need to know before I speak to my lawyer if you are going to reject the offer to sell and keep the factory open. Maybe later, if we ever do decide to redevelop,' she continued, warming to her theme, 'perhaps it could be shops and a recreation centre—something that could provide other work in the community. Dessington is in a pretty part of Norfolk—not far from the coast—and it could bring in tourists much like here.'

Lorenzo listened to her with deepening distaste as she rambled on about what 'they' might do if the factory eventually did close. Enthralled by her lush body, he had almost forgotten her hated name, and the business that had brought them together. But—typical female—Lucy had not, and though she took the high moral ground, wanting to save the workers, basically she was out for every penny she could get. He had learned his lesson years ago, when he'd lived in America and found the girl he had been going to surprise with an engagement ring in bed with another man—a man she'd imagined was wealthier than him—and it was not one he would ever forget.

Women always had an agenda, and Lucy was no exception. There was no denying sex with her was incredible, though she was not as adventurous as some women he had known—sometimes even seeming shocked—and she did have a tendency to blush, which was amazing given her lifestyle. Or maybe it was just a ploy to give the impression of innocence. He didn't care, because her last appeal had confirmed his original decision. The weekend affair was over, and he had no intention of seeing her again.

'Your ideas sound admirable, Lucy, but totally misguided. There is no *we*,' he said with brutal frankness. 'I told you the first time you asked I had no intention of doing business with a Steadman again, and that has not changed.'

Lucy couldn't believe what she was hearing. She stared at him, tall, dark and remote, his eyes cold and hard, and felt as if she was looking at a stranger. 'But you said...' She stopped. It had been his suggestion they might keep the factory... She didn't understand what was happening—didn't want to. 'I thought...' What did she think? That they were friends? More than friends...? 'We made love—'

'We had sex,' Lorenzo cut in, and she was silenced by his statement. 'Something I consider more pleasure than business, but if you want to mix the two fair enough,' he drawled with a shrug of his broad shoulders. 'I will postpone selling for a month, to give you time to make other arrangements if you can.' The light, conversational tone of his voice belied the cold black eyes looking down at her, devoid of any glimmer of light.

'You will?' she murmured, but inside her heart shrivelled as the import of his words sank in. To Lorenzo they'd had sex, nothing more. Whereas she, in her inexperience, had begun to imagine it was a whole lot more—something very special—and she was halfway to falling in love with him. How could she have been so wrong?

'Yes. I don't like weddings, and avoid them whenever possible, but thanks in the most part to you, Lucy, I have rather enjoyed the weekend. In fact I'll delay the sale of Steadman's for *two* months,' he offered. 'You were really good, and cheap at the price.'

Lucy stared at him with wide, wounded eyes and dragged in a deep, agonising breath. His words sliced at her heart. She had never been so insulted in her life, and she fought back the pain that threatened to double her over. That he could actually think she had made love to him simply to get him to agree a deal over Steadman's horrified her—but then she recalled Lorenzo had thought the same the first time he had kissed her in his office. His mindset had never altered. He was still a power-wielding, cynical banker, to whom money was everything and everything had a price—including her. His insinuation that he might hang onto the factory had been nothing more than a ploy to soften her up and get her into bed, but if he thought she would be grateful that he was postponing the sale he had got the wrong girl.

When not blinded by love—no, not love, *sex,* Lucy amended, she was a bright, intelligent woman. Suddenly the pain gave way to fury, and she started to raise her hand, wanting to lash out at him, then stopped. Violence was never an answer, but his insinuation that he was paying for her services had cut her to the bone. Lorenzo had used her, but it was her own dumb fault for letting him. He actually *was* the ruthless devil his brother had said, and yet she still could not quite believe it.

'Why?' Lucy asked. 'Why are you behaving like an immoral jerk?'

'Oh, please—don't pretend you are Miss Morality, Lucy. You enjoyed the sex as much as I did,' he informed her, with an arrogantly inclined head, his glittering dark eyes looking down at her contemptuously. 'You are exactly like your brother—up for anything at any cost. And *your* brother cost mine his life.'

'But it was an accident,' she said, confused by the change of subject.

'So the coroner said—but I believe what your brother did was contemptible...tantamount to manslaughter,' Lorenzo stated, but he saw no reason to prolong the conversation by getting into the details with Lucy. It was over and done with, and he was finished with her. 'So now you know why I have no desire to do business with Steadman's. I will *never* forgive and forget—is that plain enough for you?'

Lucy was stunned by the antagonism in his voice. She had not been mistaken when they'd met in his office and she had the thought his refusal was personal...it *had* been. Her face paled as the full weight of his contempt hit her, and anger almost choked her.

'Yes,' she said coldly. 'I always knew, but I forgot for a while.' Her slender hands clenched at her sides to prevent the urge to claw his devious eyes out. She'd had no chance from the start, she realised bitterly. If the only reason Lorenzo had had sex with her was some perverted form of revenge or payback for her brother's perceived behaviour, she didn't know—and cared less. All she *did* know was she was not taking it lying down.

'Damien told me what you said to him after the inquest, blaming him for what happened, but foolishly—knowing how it feels to lose someone you love—when I met you I decided anger and grief had maybe made you act out of character. I gave you the benefit of the doubt, but now I see how wrong I was. You really are a ruthless devil. But I *am* holding you to your promise of two months' reprieve. As you so succinctly put it, I have paid for it—with sex.' And, spinning on her heel, she walked into the house, slamming the door behind her.

Lorenzo was stunned for a moment. The fact she

knew about his confrontation with her brother had shocked him—though it was not really so surprising when he thought about it. Not that it mattered any more. He was never going to see her again. He got in the car and left.

Quivering with rage and humiliation, Lucy threw her keys down on the table in the entrance hall and dashed up the stairs to her flat, trying to ignore Lorenzo's hateful insults. But every time she thought of him—thought of what she had done with him—she felt cheap and dirty.

She ripped off her clothes and headed straight for the shower, ashamed and angry. Lorenzo had as good as called her a whore, and she wanted to wash every trace of him off her body. But perversely that same body remembered every touch, every caress.

Maybe she was fated to be ashamed every time she had sex, she thought hysterically, and finally she crawled into bed and let the tears fall, crying until she had no tears left.

Monday morning Lucy woke from a brief tormented sleep, hugging her pillow. For a second she inhaled the scent of Lorenzo, and smiled. Then reality hit, and she dragged herself out of bed, telling herself she must change the sheets. She staggered into the bathroom and groaned when she looked in the mirror. Her eyes were red and swollen from the tears she had shed over Lorenzo Zanelli, and however much she tried to convince herself he wasn't worth a second thought her body ached for him with every breath she took.

Showered, and dressed in cotton pants and a tee shirt, she stood in the gallery, a cup of coffee in her hand, and glanced around. Usually it gave her pleasure, looking over her little kingdom before anyone arrived. She was proud of what she had accomplished. But today she didn't get the same thrill.

'Hi, Lucy.'

Lucy drained her coffee cup and tried to smile as Elaine walked in with a spring in her step, ready to start the working week—before she took in her friend's face.

'My God, that must have been some night. I know you rarely drink, but you look like you have a one hell of a hangover.'

'No, nothing like that,' Lucy said. 'Much worse.'

'Do tell all.' Elaine tilted Lucy's head up with a finger and really stared at her. 'You look different, and you have been crying. That can only mean one thing—man trouble. I thought yesterday you looked remarkably happy, but we were so busy I never got to ask you why. What happened last night? Discovered he was married, did you?'

'Discovered he was only interested in a dirty weekend,' Lucy said bitterly, but couldn't bring herself to tell Elaine the whole story.

'Lucy, you are far too naïve where men are concerned. Stop beating yourself up because you were finally tempted by sex—you've never had a lover as long as I've known you, and it was way past time you did. Put it down to experience and get over it. You are not the first and won't be the last. Weddings are notorious for causing brief affairs. Too much champagne and the best man gets off with the bridesmaid, the guests get off with each other. One wedding Sid and I went to the *bridegroom* actually got off with the bridesmaid—needless to say the marriage only lasted the length of the honeymoon, when the happy couple returned home and the bride found out.'

'I don't believe it.' Lucy actually managed a weak smile.

'Ask Sid—the groom was an acquaintance of his. He told me the man was a serial womaniser and I didn't believe him, but he was right.'

'Okay, you've made your point. Actually, when I first met Lorenzo I didn't like him, and my original impression was he was no gentleman. I should have trusted my instincts and steered clear. He certainly proved me right.'

'Good—you are seeing him for the rat he obviously is, and that is the first step to recovery. Now, put the experience behind you and get on with your life. I'll take over here and you can spend the day in your studio, creating your next great masterpiece or making a start on your latest commission. If you stay here you will scare the customers.'

Lucy agreed—not that she felt like painting. All she wanted to do was forget the weekend had ever happened. She took out her sketchbook and began to draw, but to her dismay found the small boy's face she was copying had morphed into a remarkable likeness of Lorenzo.

She looked at it for a long time and then, turning the page of her sketchpad, began again. Art had always been her release valve from any pressure in life, and before long she was totally immersed in her work.

The next day her lawyer called and confirmed that the sale of Steadman's had been postponed for two months. So Lorenzo had done what he promised. He was a cynical devil to pay for her favours in such a way, but at least it gave her some time to figure something out for the factory. On the sketch she had started yesterday she coloured the eyes red and added horns, whiskers and a tail...

Somehow it was cathartic, thinking of him that way. Whenever Lucy felt really down, her body hot and aching, her mind tormented by images of him making love to her, she would only have to look at the sketch to remind herself what a devil...a love-rat...he really was.

'At last you look more like yourself,' Elaine declared, walking into the gallery on Saturday morning three weeks later and eyeing Lucy up and down. 'That turquoise dress Leon brought back from India is gorgeous—the colour really suits you, and the beading is perfect. But go upstairs and take that braid out of your hair and leave it loose. Remember you are a beautiful, highly talented artist, and when you try you can sell anything and everything. I have a feeling we are going to have a great day today.'

Lucy laughed. 'I'm not sure that is a compliment to my paintings.' But she did as Elaine said, and went upstairs and unbraided her hair. She stood in front of the mirror, brushing her hair back from her brow and fastening it with a silver clip, then brushed the long length down to tumble over her shoulders in gentle waves. Slowly it dawned on her that Elaine was right. The pale, sad-eyed reflection of the last few weeks was gradually fading.

Last night she had taken a walk down into the centre of Looe, and as she'd strolled along the harbour through the crowd of happy holidaymakers she'd been reminded of how much she had loved the place from the very first time her parents had brought her here. How much she still loved the place. She'd felt her heart lift a little.

This morning, on a whim, she had put on the brightly coloured dress, and she looked more like her old self again. Picking up a lipstick, she applied it to her full lips and, smiling, added a touch of mascara to her long lashes and clipped on an earring. Business was going well, and she had enough commissions to keep her busy for a while. Life was good.

Even the trip two weeks ago she had been dreading, to clear out the family home in Dessington before putting the house on the market, had turned out to be inspirational.

Meeting old friends from school, visiting the factory and talking to the workers, being greeted by shopkeepers and reminded how much everyone had respected her grandfather, who had started the business, and her parents, who had been socially active in the town until her mum died, had all reminded Lucy what a happy childhood she had.

The memories had helped concentrate her mind on the problem of the factory, and standing looking around the huge garden of her family home she'd had a *eureka* moment... She had come up with a brilliant idea that could save the factory and help the community.

She had spoken to her lawyer, arranging to meet Richard Johnson—the third partner in Steadman's—and had pitched her proposition to him. He was not the ogre she had imagined, and after a productive meeting with him and his architect, and subject to the approval of the town council, they had agreed on a very different deal. Lucy had made the necessary arrangements with her bank, and also a telephone call from her new partner yesterday it was virtually a done deal. What gave her the most satisfaction was the fact she had achieved everything without any help from the despicable Zanelli.

Deep down Lucy had always known Lorenzo was not for her. In every respect they were poles apart—in temperament and aspiration, and in culture... He was a billionaire banker, devoted to making more money, with centuries of tradition behind him making him the arrogant, cynical man he was. Her life was her art and her friends. Money didn't bother her so long as the bills were paid and her conscience was clear.

Unlike Lorenzo, who didn't *have* a conscience, she thought. And later she was to be proved absolutely right...

## CHAPTER FIVE

LORENZO had extended his stay in New York to three weeks, and had on his return to Italy last night found, as expected, the Olivia Paglia rumours had faded away—problem solved. This morning he had agreed to his mother's request to have dinner with her tonight, as he had not visited in over a month. And now he had an even bigger problem that was a hell of a lot harder to solve.

He glanced at his mother across the dining table. He hadn't seen her so animated in years, but the reason for it exasperated him. He glanced down again at the handful of photographs spread on the table. Teresa Lanza had presented them to his mother, along with the information that the girl in the picture was none other than Lucy Steadman. How had he hoped to keep that quiet, with the Lanza family in attendance? He must have been out of his mind.

'Why did you not tell me, Lorenzo? You let me scold you about that Paglia woman and all this time you had a lovely girlfriend—a talented artist, no less. Was it because you thought I might be upset because of her relationship to Damien? You need not have worried. I remember Antonio telling me about Damien's sister—he thought she was a lovely girl. Antonio and Damien were such great friends, and I never blamed Damien for the tragic accident. As the coroner said, he did the right thing to try and save Antonio's life.' She sighed. 'It was just a pity the rescue services were too late.'

Lorenzo stiffened in his chair, his lips twisting in a cynical smile. He didn't agree, but there was no point arguing so he ignored her last comment. 'I do not have girlfriends, Mother. I have female partners occasionally, and Lucy Steadman is neither. I barely know her, so drop the subject.'

'Oh, dear!' she said, and he caught a slightly guilty look on her face before she continued. 'Well, that is not the impression Teresa got. She showed me all the photos they took of you and Lucy together at the wedding, and it was very good of her to make these copies for me. Teresa said you seemed very close, and you told her you had known Lucy for quite a while. She also told me that Lucy has no family left—her father died, and then her brother last year. She is all alone in the world. You could have told me, Lorenzo.'

He picked up his wine glass and drained it in one gulp. 'I did not know myself until recently,' he said, appalled at the way the conversation was going. 'As for Teresa Lanza, she must have misunderstood me. I never said I had known Lucy for quite a while. I said I had known *of her* for a while. I have met her twice— once at the wedding, and once before that on business.' Thinking fast, he saw an opportunity to rid himself of at least one problem and explain to his mother why it made sense to sell the shares in Steadman's.

'As you apparently know, Lucy Steadman is an artist. She has no interest in plastics whatsoever. She was in Verona recently, to deliver a painting, and at her re- quest we had a meeting at the bank to discuss the sale of Steadman Industrial Plastics. I didn't mention it to you in case it upset you. I know how pleased you were about Antonio investing in the firm, planning for the future, and you may have wanted the bank to hang on to Steadman's for sentimental reasons that make no financial sense to the other partners.'

'Oh! You're right—I would have liked to keep the link to Antonio, so I can understand your reasoning. But I see now selling is the obvious thing to do. Tying an artist to a plastics factory is laughable. In fact I want you to ask her here for a visit.'

Lorenzo could not believe what he was hearing. 'Why on earth would you want to do that?' he asked, barely hiding his astonishment.

'Why—to offer her my condolences on the loss of her brother and father, of course. I should have done it long ago. Besides which, if I met Lucy I could commission her to paint a portrait of Antonio. By all accounts the portrait she has done of the Contessa della Scala's husband is wonderful. So you will ask her for me?'

It was more of a command than a request, but one he had no intention of fulfilling.

'As I said, Mamma, I hardly know the girl. But what I do know is she is dedicated to her work and runs an art and craft gallery in Cornwall. The summer is her busiest period, so she could not get away even if she wanted. And I don't know her well enough to ask.'

'Lorenzo, I am not so old I can't recognise a lover's kiss—and if you don't ask her I will. I'll ring her. You must have her phone number…or the bank will.'

The hell of it was his mother would. She might be frail, but she had a stubborn streak. Suddenly Lorenzo realised his weekend affair was in danger of becoming a millstone around his neck, and he had no one to blame but himself… He had been so intent on getting Lucy into bed all his thinking had been concentrated below the belt. His innate control and common sense had flown out of the window.

Silently he cursed. It had never entered his head that the Lanzas would take pictures of the wedding guests. There was one of him with his arm lodged firmly around Lucy's waist while they talked, and the most damning of all had to be Aldo's work—it was him kissing Lucy in the garden, just before the man had interrupted them...

'We were not lovers. It was too much champagne and a friendly kiss—that is all. But all right...I'll call Lucy,' he conceded, and left shortly after.

Back in his apartment, Lorenzo stood by the window, looking out over the city without actually seeing it, a glass of whisky in his hand. Antonio, as the baby of the family, had been his mother's favourite, though she had tried not to show it, and with hindsight Lorenzo recognised Antonio had been indulged by all of them. He knew his mother was not likely to give up on the idea of meeting Lucy and commissioning a portrait of Antonio any time soon... He crossed the room and flopped down on the sofa, draining his glass and putting it on the table. Whisky was not the answer.

The hell of it was Lorenzo could not see a way out of the situation without involving Lucy Steadman.

Basically he had two options. He could do as his mother asked and mention commissioning a portrait of Antonio to Lucy, invite her to visit his mother. The big flaw in that scenario was that Lucy knew of his run-in with Damien, which he wished to keep from his mother. She had been hurt enough, and didn't need bitterness added to her memories. The whole idea was a non-starter as far as he was concerned.

He had cut Lucy out of his life and wanted it to stay that way—and after the brutal way he had left her he was sure she would refuse any invitation from him point-blank. But if by some fluke Lucy *did* accept, he had no doubt as a woman scorned she would take great delight in telling his mother of his run-in with Damien just to spite him. A ruthless gleam sparked in his dark eyes. That was never going to happen—because Lucy wasn't going to get the chance.

The second option—the one that appealed to his cynical mind and which, with his experience of women, he knew would succeed—was the only option. He would offer Lucy a big fat bribe. He would give her the bank's shares in Steadman's in return for her refusing any overtures his mother might make and for her silence on the accident if she did contact her.

Lucy had disturbed his peace of mind long enough. He had taken an old girlfriend out to dinner in New York and given her only a goodnight kiss when she had been expecting a whole lot more—as had he until he'd realised he felt no inclination to take the stunning brunette back to his apartment or anywhere else.

Lucy had wanted him to vote with her on the Steadman's deal. Well, this way she could have the shares outright and do what the hell she liked with them. The money was nothing to him, and he had wasted far too much of his time dwelling on Lucy Steadman as it was. Finally all connection with the despised family would be severed for good.

He flicked on his cell phone to dial Lucy's number, having got it from the bank and entered it in his speed dial, and then stopped. She would certainly hang up on him. Better to catch her by surprise, even though it meant he would have to see her again. Definitely for the last time, he told himself, and ignored the stirring in his body at the thought...

Instead he rang his lawyer, and told him what he needed by morning.

'Lucy!' Elaine cried, and dashed into the small kitchen at the back of the gallery, where Lucy was standing with the teapot in her hand, about to pour out a couple of much needed cups of tea, after a very successful day's trading, to enjoy while they closed up.

'What's the panic? A late influx of customers?' Lucy queried.

'No—just one. A man asking for you. I can see now why you were so upset over the Lorenzo guy. Scumbag he may be, but he is here—and what a hunk. I bet he is great in bed. Not that I'm suggesting you should make the same mistake again.'

Lucy paled, then blushed, then paled again, her stomach churning at the thought of seeing Lorenzo again.

'Go,' Elaine said, taking the teapot from her hand and pushing her towards the hall. 'Get rid of him—and if you need help call me.'

She didn't need help—not any more, not on any level. She was over him. But that didn't stop the painful details of the last time they'd been together flashing through her mind. Why he was back she didn't know—and didn't want to know. He could not have made it plainer: he'd used her, paid her, and despised her simply for who she was.

Straightening her shoulders and flicking her hair back from her face, Lucy walked down the hall, determination in every step she took. She would not allow any man to use her and walk over her ever again...

Lorenzo appeared in the open doorway of the gallery

and her heart lurched at the sight of him. She hesitated. He was casually dressed, in a white linen shirt open at the throat and washed denim jeans that hung low on his hips and clung to his muscular thighs like a second skin—designer, no doubt, she thought, and glanced up. Her green eyes clashed with deep brown, and it took every ounce of will-power she possessed to hold his gaze as her traitorous heart pounded like a drum in her chest.

'Lucy.' He said her name, and smiled the same slightly rueful but sensual smile that had seduced her before. But she was wiser now, and wasn't fooled.

'Mr Zanelli,' she responded, walking forward. He was so confident she would fall into his arms—she could see it in his eyes, in the arrogant tilt of his head, and felt anger stir deep within her...along with a more basic emotion which she battled to ignore. 'This is a surprise. I never expected to see you again. Come to buy a painting?' she suggested facetiously.

'No, I've come to see you. We need to talk.'

'No, we don't. I have no interest in anything you say.'

'Not even if it means saving Steadman's?' Lorenzo prompted, sure that would tempt her. But he was sorely tempted himself, and the sudden tightening in his groin was a reminder of how much.

He had flown into Newquay Airport, barely an hour's drive away, and he had every intention of returning to Italy tonight. The sooner the better. He hadn't slept with a woman since Lucy, and the strain was getting to him.

Every time he saw her she was different—from bag lady to gowned elegance to young and sexy in a skimpy summer dress. Today she was an exotic vision in a plunging necked shimmering turquoise silk eastern thing, with a beaded band beneath her high firm breasts and a skirt that swirled around her feet. Some of her glorious hair was swept back in a clip on top of her head, and the rest fell in a silken mass down over her shoulders. In one ear she was wearing the most amazing huge silver spiderweb earring, with long white feathers attached that floated down against the curve of a breast. As for her mouth—her lips were painted a vibrant pink, and so full and sensually promising he ached to taste them and a whole lot more. Never, even as a teenager with rampant hormones, had he ever felt such a need to kiss a woman.

'No, thank you.' Lucy said bluntly.

Dragging his gaze from her lips, Lorenzo saw the anger in her eyes and realised what she had said. 'A polite refusal, but not a very sensible one—or business-like,' he prompted, and moved closer. He could see the pulse beating in her slender neck. She was not as cool as she would have him believe.

'You once told me I should stay out of business and you were right. The way you do business is despicable and the cost far too high for any self-respecting person. Now, I must ask you to leave—we are about to close.' Lucy walked to the front door and flipping the sign to 'Closed', held the door open. 'This is the way out.'

She glanced back at Lorenzo. He stood where she had left him, his dark eyes narrowed angrily on her face, then in two lithe strides he was beside her. His hand reached out to circle her throat and he tipped her head back. Shocked, she grasped his wrist with her free hand to pull his hand away.

'You didn't find me despicable when you were naked beneath me on the bed, moaning my name.' He brushed his lips lightly against hers and laid his other hand over her breast. To her shame, her lips stung and her nipple tightened beneath his palm. 'And it wouldn't take me five minutes to get you that way again, Lucy,' he taunted her softly.

Lorenzo was so damned arrogant—and yet possessed of a vibrant sexuality that could heat up a room and every woman in it, Lucy thought helplessly. He was almost irresistible, but resist him she did, her pulse-rate rising with her anger at the insult. She dug her nails hard into his wrist and he let go of her throat. She let go of the door and did what she should have done weeks ago. Bringing her hand up, she struck him as hard as she could across the face, catching him unawares. Her hand cracked against his cheek and rocked him back on his heels. The heavy door caught his shoulder.

Lucy, chest heaving in outrage, stepped back into the hall and spun round to face him. 'You have a mind like a sewer. Sex and money is all you think about!' she yelled, her green eyes spitting with rage. 'That is exactly what I would expect from you and you got exactly what you deserved.'

'Hey, Lucy?' Elaine called out as she appeared in the hall. 'Is everything okay?'

Appalled by her loss of temper, Lucy stared at Lorenzo's cheek, with the imprint of her fingers clearly visible, and then at Elaine. 'Yes, it's fine,' she said, and took a deep steadying breath, forcing a smile to her lips. She did not want to involve Elaine. 'Mr Zanelli and I had a discussion, that is all.'

'We still are, Lucy,' Lorenzo inserted, reining in the furious impulse to shake her till she rattled. What was it about this witch of a woman that made him lose his legendary control? He was here for one reason only, he reminded himself. He could fob his mother off for a while, but he was taking no chances—and he needed Lucy to agree to have nothing to do with his mother if she *did* call. Especially if she tried to commission a painting that would keep Lucy Steadman on the periphery of his life for heaven knew how long.

But holding her by the throat was no way to go about it.

He turned to the other woman, slightly taller and a lot wider than Lucy. 'Elaine, isn't it?' he said smoothly, his razor-sharp brain quickly recalling Lucy's explanation that Elaine, who did tapestries, also helped out at the shop. 'Don't concern yourself. Lucy and I got our wires crossed—I believe that is the English expression—but it is nothing we cannot put right, I assure you.'

'That does not look like a wire that crossed your face,' Elaine quipped. 'More like a hand—and it serves you right. A married man should know better than to mess around with a single woman.'

Elaine's witty comment in rushing to her defence cooled Lucy's anger—then she realised she had by omission misled her friend.

Lorenzo's cheek was stinging, and he had probably bruised his shoulder, but he could have sworn his head was clear and he was in control. Yet these two women were intent on driving him crazy—and who the hell was the married man?

'What married man?' he asked, his dark gaze skimming from Elaine to settle on Lucy and catch the guilty look on her expressive face.

Surely she had not taken up with another man already? A married one at that? Not that he cared—he was here for the express purpose of getting Lucy Steadman out of his life for good, and was prepared to pay to do so. His one regret was that he hadn't cut the Steadmans out of his family's life years ago, before her brother had talked Antonio into the reckless lifestyle that had got him killed. As for Lucy—he knew exactly what type of woman she was and yet the thought of her with another man did nothing to help his self-control.

'You, of course,' Elaine answered. 'Lucy told me all about you.'

'Did she, now?' Lorenzo said, never taking his eyes off Lucy. He saw her nervously chew her bottom lip and she would not look him in the eye. 'I'm surprised at you, Lucy. You know perfectly well I am not married—never have been, and never likely to be. Which makes me wonder what other fairytales you have told your friend,' he drawled, shaking his head mockingly. 'We really do need to talk.'

'He is *not* married?' Elaine queried, and looked at Lucy.

Lucy finally met her friend's puzzled gaze. 'Not to my knowledge—and if you recall I never said he was, Elaine. I think you must have jumped to the wrong conclusion after giving me the benefit of your own dubious wedding experiences.'

Elaine looked from Lucy to Lorenzo and back again. 'Ah, well, that is different.' She chuckled, obviously amused. 'Well, good luck, Lucy, in sorting out your problems. I'll just get my bag and leave.' And she disappeared down the hall, to reappear a minute later, with a cheery wave and a goodbye as she closed the door and left.

There was silence. Lucy glanced up and found Lorenzo's gleaming dark eyes resting on her. Something in his look made her stomach curl and she flushed hotly.

'Time for you to leave, Mr Zanelli,' she said curtly. 'We have nothing more to discuss and I need to lock up.' She glanced back at him. 'I don't want any more customers *or* uninvited visitors.'

He did not respond—didn't move. He was towering over her, intimidating her with his presence, and suddenly the hall seemed smaller. Lucy had had enough. 'Goodnight, and good riddance. Is that plain enough for you?' she mocked, parroting the words he had said to her the last time she had seen him, and she reached for the handle to open the door again.

But Lorenzo was quicker, and before she could react a strong hand had clamped around her waist and pulled her hard against his body, trapping her arm against her side while the other hand slid beneath the heavy fall of her hair to tug her head back. Deliberately he bent and pressed his mouth against the pulse that beat erratically in her throat, and she felt it like a flame.

'Don't,' she gasped, and pushed against his chest with her hand while his mouth seared up her slender neck. 'Let go of me, you great brute. I *hate* you,' she flung at him savagely.

'No, you don't.' His head came up. His eyes were black in his hard, masculine face, and Lucy could not control the slight tremor in her limbs. 'You want me. But then women like you can't help themselves,' he said contemptuously.

She punched his chest with a curled fist, but it was like hitting a brick wall. She lifted her knee and suddenly he whirled her round, making her head spin. Before she could draw breath, let alone find her feet, his head lowered, and she moaned in protest as his mouth came down hard and ruthless against her lips, forcibly parting them, demanding her surrender.

For a moment she made herself stay rigid in his arms, but then her mouth trembled in helpless response and she succumbed to the powerful passion of his kiss. When he finally released her she stumbled back and deliberately wiped her hand across her mouth, but to her shame she could not wipe away so easily the warring sensations inside her.

'You should not have done that, Mr Zanelli,' she snapped.

Lorenzo stared down at her, his broad shoulders tense, his face expressionless. 'Maybe not, but you provoked me—and if I have succeeded in shutting you up long enough to listen it was well worth it. And you can drop the "Mr Zanelli"—you know my name and you have used it too intimately to pretend otherwise. Now, we can go up to your apartment and I'll tell you why I am here.'

Lucy looked at him warily, silently conceding it *was* a bit childish calling him Mr Zanelli. Her real problem was that she didn't trust him, but short of throwing him out—which was a physical impossibility—she hadn't much choice but to listen to what he had to say.

'And it isn't what you are thinking,' he drawled, with a sardonic lift of one ebony brow. Though his body was telling him different...

'I'll listen, but not here,' Lucy conceded. 'I usually go into town on Saturday evening to eat. You can come with me.' She wanted Lorenzo out of her home and among other people—simply because her own innate honesty forced her to admit she didn't trust herself alone with him.

'My car or yours?' Lorenzo asked as, after locking up the gallery, they walked out into the front yard that doubled as a car park.

'Neither.' Lucy flicked a glance up at him. 'We can walk down the hill—it is not far.'

Stepping onto the grass verge that ran down the side of the road and Lorenzo joined her, but didn't look too comfortable when a Jeep whizzed past with a group of four young men on board.

'Hi, Lucy!' they all yelled, and waved. Lucy waved back.

'Friends of yours?' Lorenzo asked.

'Yes—students in my weekly art class at the high school. Now, why don't you start talking? I'm listening.'

Another car went by and tooted its horn, and Lucy waved again.

'No. I'd prefer to wait until we reach the restaurant,' Lorenzo said, adding, 'Less interruptions.' And more time for him to regain his self-control.

He'd had no idea she taught art—but then he did not really know her except in the biblical sense. And he didn't want to. Lucy Steadman infuriated him, enraged him and aroused him, and he did not like it—did not like *her*. But he did need her silence, and in his experience the best way to get anything from a woman was to humour her for a while—let her think she was in control...

Lucy hid a smile. He was in for a rude awakening if he was expecting a restaurant...

Lorenzo looked around with interest when they reached the main road. Set in a narrow valley, Looe was very picturesque, with a stone bridge that spanned the tidal river to the other side of town. Lucy led him down the main street that wound its way alongside the harbour and the river to the beach. He couldn't believe the number of tourists around, or the amount of people

that Lucy knew. Every few yards someone stopped her
to say hello.

He wasn't really surprised. With her long hair flowing over her shoulders, the feather-laden earring flutter-
ing in the breeze and her brilliant smile she looked like
some rare exotic butterfly. But there was no mistaking
she was a woman, and the pressure in his groin that had
plagued him from the minute he set eyes on her was
becoming a problem again…

Ten minutes later, sitting on the harbour wall, Lorenzo
glanced warily down at the box Lucy handed him, and
then at her.

'I got you pizza because you're Italian. The fish and
chip shop sells all sorts,' she said, opening the carton
containing her fish and chips.

'Thanks.' Lorenzo opened the box. 'I think…' he
drawled, eyeing what passed for a pizza in an English
holiday town with some trepidation. He didn't want to
know what the assorted toppings and cheeses were, but
it was nothing like any pizza *he* had ever seen.

'I am ready to listen, so fire away,' Lucy said, shoot-
ing Lorenzo a sidelong glance, secretly amused. He was
eyeing the pizza as if it was going to jump up and bite
him, not the other way around. How were the mighty
fallen… He must want something from her pretty badly
to lower himself to sitting on a harbour wall and eating
a takeaway pizza.

'We have a problem, Lucy.'

*There is no we* were the words that sprang to mind,
but Lucy resisted the urge to taunt him with the words he
had used the last time they were together. Let him hang
himself, she thought. There was something immensely
satisfying in knowing that whatever Lorenzo was after

he was not going to get it. Instead she picked up a chip and ate it.

'We do?' she queried. Stringing the superior devil along was going to be fun. Breaking off a piece of battered cod, she popped it in her mouth and glanced up at him with fake concern, licking her lips.

'Yes.' Lorenzo tore his gaze away from the small pink tongue running along her top lip. 'Remember the wedding?' She arched a delicate brow in his direction. Stupid question—of course she did. 'Unfortunately Teresa Lanza called in to my mother to fill her in about the wedding—including the fact that Lucy Steadman was the bridesmaid. Then she showed her the photographs she had taken—quite a few of you and I.'

'Is this story going anywhere?' Lucy cut in. She had finished her fish and chips, and she had finished with Lorenzo, but sitting close to him on the wall, with the brush of his thigh against her own, was testing her resolve to the limit. Stringing him along had lost its appeal.

'The upshot is that my mother wants me to invite you to visit her in Italy. She also wants to commission a portrait of Antonio. Obviously I don't want you anywhere near her. I can put her off for a while, but unfortunately she is determined lady. If I don't ask you she says she will ask you herself. If she does, you are to refuse any offer she makes.'

'Don't worry—I will. I'm not a masochist. Listening to *you* denigrating my brother and I was more than enough,' Lucy said and, standing up, walked along the harbour to the nearest littler bin and deposited the carton in it.

Lorenzo followed her. She noted he hadn't eaten even half the pizza as he tipped it in the bin, and wasn't surprised. But she *was* surprised he had come all this way to tell her not to speak to his mother. That hurt. As if she needed telling again how low he thought her…

She walked on.

'Wait, Lucy.' He grasped her upper arm. 'I have not finished.'

'I have,' she said flatly, glancing up at him and doing her best to ignore the warmth of his hand around her arm. 'I've got the message loud and clear. I am not usually impolite, but if by any remote chance your mother calls me I will make an exception and tell her to get lost. As you said, no contact of any kind ever again between a Steadman and a Zanelli can only be a good thing—and you can start by letting go of my arm and getting out of my life for good.'

His face darkened, and if she wasn't mistaken he looked almost embarrassed, but he did let go of her arm and she carried on walking back the way they'd come.

'I don't want you to be rude to her,' he said, walking along beside her. 'My mother does not know what I know about Damien. She believes your brother did his best to try and save Antonio, and I don't want her disillusioned and hurt again. You must make no reference whatsoever to my argument with Damien. Total silence on the subject—do you understand?'

He glanced down at her, and Lucy had the spiteful thought that he had had no problem disillusioning *her* when she had for a moment imagined herself falling in love with him, or hurting *her* feelings. Why should his mother be exempt?

'Okay, I'll let her down gently but firmly and keep silent about you,' she said, with a hint of sarcasm in her tone that went straight over his arrogant head.

'Good. I propose that you regretfully suggest any

reminder of Damien and Antonio upsets you so much
you could not possibly face the prospect of bringing it all
back—something along those lines. I'll leave the excuses
up to you—women are good at dissembling—and in
return I will give you the bank's holding in Steadman's.
Naturally my lawyer has drawn up a confidentiality
agreement that will be binding on both sides. I have it
in the car. All I need is for you to sign and it is a done
deal.'

Lorenzo obviously adored his mother, and wanted
to protect her, but he was just as controlling with the
frail little woman as he was with everything else, Lucy
thought. For a second she had been sympathetic to his
predicament of trying to save his mother from any hurt,
even though she knew he was wrong about Damien, but
his insulting comment that women were basically good
at lying, and his offer to buy her off with his bank's
share of Steadman's, had killed any sympathy she felt
stone-dead.

'I'll think about your offer as we walk back,' she
said noncommittally. But inside she was seething. He
had no qualms about deceiving his mother, albeit he
believed it to be for her own good. But that he had the
arrogance—the gall—to ask Lucy to do the same, and
say that he would pay her for her trouble, was beyond
belief. The man thought he could buy anyone and anything, from sex to silence. She almost said no. But a
grain of caution—not something she was known for—
told her that just in case anything went wrong with her
plan to save the factory she should say yes…

Lucy didn't speak to him or look at him again, but
she could feel his eyes on her—could sense the growing
tension in him with every step she took until they finally
reached her home.

'So, Lucy, do your agree?' he asked, stopping by his car.

'Yes. But with one proviso...no, two,' she amended. 'If your mother calls I will not lie to her—though I will remain silent about you and Damien and refuse any invitation she may make politely and finally.'

'Excellent.' Lorenzo smiled cynically. Money never failed. He opened the car door to get the briefcase containing the documents.

Lucy wasn't finished. 'But as far as the confidentiality agreement goes—forget it. You will have to take my word. And as for commissioning a painting...wait here a minute.'

And while Lorenzo was hastily extracting himself from the car, with a resounding bump on his proud forehead, Lucy ducked inside the house, locking the door behind her.

She made straight for her studio at the rear of the gallery, ignoring the hammering on the front door. When she found what she was looking for among the stack of paintings she looked at it for a long moment, a sad, reflective smile on her face, before picking it up. About to leave, she hesitated. Finding her sketch of Lorenzo, she took that as well.

If Lucy had learnt anything over the last twelve years it was not to dwell on the past and what might have been but to cut her losses and get on with living. Straightening her shoulders, the painting and the sketch under her arm, she retraced her steps. She opened the door to see Lorenzo bristling with anger, his fist raised and ready to knock again.

'I had not finished,' he snapped. 'Let me make it perfectly clear it is my way or no way and your proviso is not acceptable. The confidentiality agreement is a must, and non-negotiable.'

'Then forget it. I'm not interested in your seedy idea, and I am finished with you *and* your family.' Anger taking over her common sense, Lucy shoved the painting and the sketch at him. 'Here—take these and your mother won't need to call.' He was so surprised he took them. 'I don't need them or you any more. I have another partner—an honourable man.' And she slipped back in the house, slamming and locking the door behind her.

Lorenzo barely registered what she'd said. He was transfixed by the painting. It was of his brother Antonio, and it was stunning. Lucy had captured the very essence of him—the black curling hair, the sparkling eyes and the smile playing around his mouth. He looked so alive, so happy with life. It was uncanny. Lorenzo realised something else. For Lucy—who could only have been a teenager at the time—to have painted this, she must have been half in love with her subject.

Then he turned the sketch over, and stilled. The painting was all light and warmth, but the sketch was the opposite—dark and red-eyed. There was no mistaking the facial likeness to him, and the little witch had added horns above the ears, and a tail. The tail was long and a given—because the sketch was a caricature of Lorenzo as a huge black rat...

Certainly not one for the family gallery or his mother...but under the circumstances it was amusing, he conceded wryly. Then her parting comment registered, and all trace of amusement faded as a cold dark fury consumed him.

Lorenzo glanced at the house, his eyes hard as jet, and debated trying again. No, next time he would be better prepared—and there would *be* a next time...

Never mind the fact he could not trust Lucy, or that she had slapped him, or that she had insulted him with the sketch. What really enraged him was that she actually had the colossal nerve to think for a second she could outsmart him in a business deal.

He needed to know the identity of this *honourable man*—the mystery benefactor who had obviously convinced Lucy he could help her save Steadman's. So much so she had turned down *his* offer with a spectacularly original gesture. He would make damn sure she lived to regret it.

Lorenzo spent the Sunday at his villa at Santa Margherita and went sailing for a few hours, having assured his mother over the phone that he had spoken to Lucy but she was too busy to visit. He said he was sure he could persuade her to do the portrait if she left it with him.

Relaxed and feeling much more like his usual self, he flew out to New York on Monday, having set in motion his investigation into the Steadman's deal, but no longer sure he was going to do anything about it.

He would sell the shares on the allotted date, as planned, and give his mother the painting in a few weeks. That would satisfy her and put an end to the whole affair.

He returned two weeks later. On entering the outer office he saw his secretary smiling widely. She presented him with the new edition of a monthly society magazine, opened at the centre page.

'Nice wedding. I recognised the bridesmaid—your new girlfriend, apparently—but I never would have suspected what was under that black suit. What a body—

lucky you!' She grinned. 'And the report you requested is on your desk.'

'What the hell?' He swore and grabbed the magazine, groaning at the headline: 'English wedding for Signor Aldo Lanza's nephew, James Morgan.' Then there were two pages of pictures of the bridal party, including Lucy, smiling broadly, and all the Italian guests, with accompanying names and captions. In one, Lucy was pinned to his side. She looked stunning, smiling up at him with her small hand resting on his shirt-front, and he was grinning down at her. The intimacy of the shot was undeniable, and the caption read: 'Lorenzo Zanelli with the bridesmaid, a long-time friend and companion.'

He read some more, then stormed into his office, slamming the door behind him.

He sat down behind his desk, fuming. The brief scandal of being linked to Olivia, a married woman, paled into nothing compared to this. Of course they had connected Lucy to her brother and resurrected the tragic accident in detail. As if he needed reminding of it...

It was all the fault of Teresa Lanza, but there was not a damn thing he could do about it. Now he knew why his mother had looked so guilty. She must have known this was coming out. The wedding had been too late in June to make the July edition, but it had certainly made the August one.

He threw it to one side and picked up the report on Steadman's. By the time he'd read it he was so enraged he slammed down the document and leapt to his feet, the deadly light of battle in his eyes. This was no longer anything to do with business or family, but strictly personal...

If there was one thing Lorenzo revelled in it was a challenge—be it at sea, sailing his yacht, or in the world of high finance—and now Lucy had become a real challenge. Pacing the floor, he realised he had seriously underestimated her. Far from being not cut out for business, she had come up with a plan to save Steadman's—and it was very imaginative and economically sound. Any bank—including his—would judge it a decent investment and back the venture.

To be beaten by a slip of a woman was unthinkable to him. Lucy had effectively sidelined him as a partner in Steadman's, and the factory was to stay open. The housing development and much more was to be built at the opposite side of town, in seven acres taken from the eight-acre river frontage garden of the house Lucy owned, in a deal she had made with Richard Johnson the property developer and third partner in Steadman's. Between them, they had the majority.

Whether she had slept with the man or not he didn't know—and didn't care. She was clever—he'd give her that—but better men and women than her had tried and failed to outsmart him, and there was no way she was getting away with it.

A few telephone calls later Lorenzo had left the bank and boarded his private Lear jet to Newquay Airport, a ruthless gleam of triumph in his dark eyes. A car and driver waited for him when his plane landed. He was back in his normal ruthless business mode, and about to make Lucy an offer she could not refuse…

# CHAPTER SIX

LUCY put down the telephone and walked slowly back into the gallery, her mind in turmoil. The call had been from Mr Johnson, her partner in the development deal. He had pulled out. No real explanation had been given—just a terse comment that he was not interested in doing business with her any more and then he'd hung up. She'd tried to ring back but the cell had gone directly to messages.

Monday was usually a slow day, and she was on her own. Much as she wanted to go upstairs and scream at the devastating news she had received she couldn't.

In between serving customers she racked her brains, trying to find a solution. She called her lawyer, who was as shocked at the news as she was, but told her he would make some enquiries and find out exactly what had happened and get back to her. She called her bank and they were no help—other than to remind her she now had to pay the mortgage on two properties.

By five-thirty Lucy had run out of ideas...

A little old lady was wandering around the pottery exhibits, and Lucy made herself walk across and ask if she could help. Five minutes later she had wrapped a hand-painted vase and taken the money, and watched as the lady left. Wearily she rubbed her back and, head spinning, sank down on the seat behind the till. Automatically she began to count the day's takings.

Now what was she going to do? she asked herself, eying the cash. Ordinarily she would have considered it a good day, but as she had taken a mortgage out on the gallery, because the bank had insisted on her having capital available up-front before considering the development loan, she was now in serious trouble.

She heard the sound of footsteps on the polished wood floor and her head whipped up. When she saw who it was all the breath was sucked from her body, her pulse racing almost as much as her mind.

'You!' she exclaimed, rising to her feet, unable to tear her eyes away from the man walking towards her. Lorenzo. There was nothing casual about him today. He was wearing an expertly tailored navy suit, and she knew by his hard, expressionless face that there was nothing casual about his visit.

Inexplicably a shiver of fear snaked down her spine.

'Lucy.' He said her name and his eyes looked straight into hers. She saw the glint of triumph in the dark depths and she knew...

'It was you,' she said, her lips twisting bitterly, anger nearly choking her. 'You got to Mr Johnson didn't you? You bastard...'

'Such language, Lucy. Really, that is no way to do business—your customers would be horrified. I told you once before business is not your thing, but I have to concede you gave it a damn good try. Your plan was excellent, but did you really think for one minute I would allow you to get the better of me?' he demanded, with an arrogant arch of one dark eyebrow.

'You *admit* it was you?' she said, horrified and furious.

'Yes. I made your new partner an offer he could not refuse,' he said, and turned round to stroll to the front door. She thought he was leaving, but instead he locked the door and turned back, staring at her with narrowed eyes, his expression unreadable. 'I've warned you before about security. You really should not sit counting money on your own. Any sneak thief could come in and rob you.'

'Like you,' she spat. 'Robbing me of Steadman's.'

Her anger drained away as the enormity of her predicament hit her. Lorenzo must have bought out Richard Johnson, so he was now the major shareholder in Steadman's and he would certainly close the factory.

'But why?' she asked, shaking her head. 'We were still going to buy you out on the agreed date, at a profit you told me yourself was good. You'd have been finished with Steadman's for ever—just what you always wanted.' She didn't understand…

'Not quite.' His eyes scanned provocatively down her shapely body, making her remember things she had fought hard to forget without much success. Colour rose in her cheeks as he walked towards her. 'I want more, Lucy.' His smile was chilling.

'More money?' she asked. 'But that does not make any sense. Buying out Mr Johnson must have cost you money, and you wanted to sell to make more money— or so you told me to up the offer the first time we met.' Lucy was no financial genius, as Lorenzo purportedly was, but even she could see the huge flaw in his deal.

'No, not money,' he said, his dark eyes fixed intently on her flushed face. 'A drink will do for a start. But upstairs—in comfort.' He made a sweeping gesture with his hand. 'After you,' he said, mocking her.

'No,' she said defiantly. 'I can find another partner…'

Even as she said the words she knew it was futile. Lorenzo now held all the cards.

'You already have, Lucy—me. I told you once before it was my way or no way. You obviously didn't listen.'

She didn't bother to answer. There was no point.

She turned back to the till, suddenly bone-weary, all the fight draining out of her, and mechanically finished cashing up. She locked the till and with the money in her hand walked past Lorenzo and upstairs to her apartment. She went straight to the bookcase that held the safe and put the cash inside, aware that he had followed her but helpless to do anything about it.

'Not much of a safe,' Lorenzo said as she locked it and, straightening up, turned back towards him.

Lucy drove him crazy. He had felt his body react the moment he'd walked in the door and seen her wearing a pair of denim shorts and a red open-necked shirt. Try as he might to control himself, seeing Lucy bending over the damn safe had almost crippled him. She had caused him more trouble than any woman he had ever known, had got under his skin for far too long, and yet he still lusted after her. He could not leave her alone, and now he was no longer going to try.

'It suits me,' Lucy responded. The security or otherwise of her house was the least of her problems under the circumstances. The immediate threat to her safety being Lorenzo. 'Take a seat. I'll get you some tea or coffee—I have nothing stronger.'

'Wait,' Lorenzo snapped and, grasping her shoulders, yanked her hard against him.

She looked up at him, and her eyes widened when they met his. What she saw in the black depths made her shiver with fear—she hoped it was fear... She tried to struggle free, but with insulting ease a strong arm swept around her back and his hand grasped her waist, holding her tight as his long fingers threaded through her hair to grip the back of her head in the palm of his hand.

A shocked gasp escaped her as she caught a glimpse of the naked desire in his dark eyes, then his mouth crashed down on hers. She raised her hands to push him away, but it was a useless gesture. His chest was as hard as marble—but a lot warmer, she realised without wanting to. She couldn't move, couldn't think. All she could do was feel as he kissed her with a demanding passion that ignited a spark deep in her belly.

Suddenly it burst into flame and her traitorous body was suffused with heat. Involuntarily she parted her lips to the hungry demand of his, her hands stroking over his chest and her body swaying into his in willing surrender. It had been so long, too long, and she could deny it no longer. She wanted Lorenzo—wanted him totally...

He lifted his head and stepped back. His hands fell from her and she was free.

'The chemistry is still there, as electric as ever, and that is all I needed to know.' She heard his deep voice as if from a distance—heard the hint of mockery as he added, 'I'll have that coffee now.'

Shamed by her body's betrayal, she closed her eyes for a moment as the heat drained out of her. When she opened them she looked at Lorenzo. His expression was hard and uncompromising. She was tempted to ask him why he was really here, but she didn't really want to know the answer because she had a horrible suspicion she would not like it.

'Okay,' she murmured, too shaken to argue, and, turning on her heel, she headed for the kitchen.

Making the coffee gave her a chance to recover from the body shock that had made her melt in his arms. She tried to tell herself her resistance was low because she was tired and Lorenzo had caught her off guard, it would never happen again, but not with any great conviction.

She returned to the living room five minutes later, a mug of instant coffee in each hand. Lorenzo had removed his jacket and tie and opened the top few buttons of his shirt. He was lounging back on her one and only sofa, looking as if he owned the place.

He glanced at her as she walked towards him, and reached out to take the coffee mug in his hand without saying a word.

It occurred to Lucy that tipping it over his head might give her some satisfaction, but resisted the urge and handed it to him. Her impulsive ideas had got her into more than enough trouble over the years, but her leap into property development had to be the biggest doozy yet. If only the bank had not been quite so briskly efficient in giving her a mortgage on this place. If only she had not been so quick to transfer the cash to the partnership to secure the development deal. Then it wouldn't be so bad.

*If only* were the saddest words in the world...

She crossed to sit down in a battered old Art Deco-style chair she had been going to re-cover for ages but never got round to, and, taking a sip of her coffee, glanced around her home. But for how much longer?

Lorenzo was right about the factory. It only just about broke even, and after the taxes were paid there was little or no profit. So basically the only income she had was from the gallery, which barely covered the two mortgages she'd have to pay until she sold the house in

Dessington. Any delay in selling and she'd very quickly go bust, she knew.

A frustrated sigh escaped her.

'That was a big sigh, Lucy. Something troubling you?'

She cast Lorenzo, her nemesis, a furious look. Lost in her troubled thoughts, she had not realised his heavy-lidded eyes were narrowed, assessing her much like a spider studied a fly caught in its web, she thought, as he smiled.

'I suppose you find it amusing, trying to wreck my plans. Excuse me if I do not.'

'Not trying—I have done,' he said, draining his coffee and cup and placing it on the occasional table. He straightened up. 'Fifty five percent of Steadman's now belongs to me. I can keep it open or shut it down. The decision is mine. As for your aspirations to develop the land adjacent to your old home—that depends on me also. Apparently your friendly lawyer called a town meeting to reassure the people and the workers you and Johnson had agreed not to close the factory. He went on to explain how a new development had been proposed and it was going to be sited in some of the eight acres of garden at your family home, donated very generously by you. That was a big mistake, Lucy.'

'I don't think so,' she muttered.

'Ah, Lucy—you should stick to art. Trust me, finance is really not your thing,' he said bluntly. 'Have you heard the term "asset-rich but cash-poor"? That is now you—because you have two mortgaged properties and a factory that makes little money and you cannot sell. The land you own could have been sold or even leased, but instead you've given away your only asset,' he drawled mockingly, casting a blatantly suggestive glance over her body before continuing. 'The outlined plan is for luxury housing, shops, a swimming pool and sports centre, and some less expensive housing to be available only for locals to purchase. The development to be named the Delia Steadman Park in honour of your mother. The whole town was delighted, apparently.'

'How on earth do you know all this?' Lucy asked.

'I made it my business to know,' he said, rising to his feet and pacing the length of the room. He turned and stopped beside her chair, staring down at her.

Refusing to be cowed, she met his dark eyes head-on. They were unreadable, and she placed her coffee mug on the floor as an excuse to look away from his harshly attractive face.

'I also know that—unlike when *I* asked you, Lucy— this time you *did* sign a legally drawn-up partnership agreement with your developer friend. But your small-town lawyer—who is, by the way, really more interested in his position as town mayor than lawyer—omitted to make it non-negotiable, and Johnson sold out to me. I am now your partner in everything except the mortgaged house in Dessington and this gallery, which you have also foolishly mortgaged. By my reckoning you won't have this much longer.'

It was worse than she'd thought, and she looked up at him again. A cruel, sardonic smile twisted his mouth.

'I'm sure I don't have to spell it out to a woman like you what that means. I own you—for as long as I want.'

A woman like her... Was there no end to his insults? Her shocked glance saw his eyes were no longer unreadable. She recognised all too well the emotion that now blazed in them: dark desire, barely leashed.

'And I *do* want you, Lucy,' he said, and she could not

suppress the shiver of revulsion his comment caused. An imp of devilment in her head defied her to name it for what it really was—excitement, desire, anticipation...

He stared down into her face, reading her reaction, and his hands reached for her, sliding under her arms. He lifted her bodily out of the chair, holding her high, her feet not touching the ground, and involuntarily she clutched at his shoulders to steady herself.

His smile was cruel. 'Ah, that's better,' he said, putting her down and moving his hands around her back, drawing her closer.

The layer of fabric between them was no protection against the shower of electric sensations that tumbled through her at the feel of his warm muscular chest against her breasts, his flat stomach and muscular thighs as he slowly lowered her down his long body to her feet. Aware of his arousal, she gasped and tried to wriggle free. But his hands tightened on her hips in a grip of iron and hauled her hard against him.

'Feel what you do to me and know what you are going to do for me.' He deliberately ground his hips against her, enflaming her senses, but she made her hands fall to her sides rather than touch him as they ached to do, all her will-power going into fighting her own rising need.

His hands lifted from her hips to link lightly around her back, and she managed to draw away a little from the seductive warmth of his great body—but not free. She had a sinking sensation she might never be free of him...

He watched her. She could feel the intensity of his dark eyes even though she'd averted her face. And then he resumed speaking in a clipped tone, as though addressing some underling.

'You, Lucy, will be my lover whenever I want you. And you will do exactly as I tell you on the single occasion you will visit my mother.'

'Visit? Why? I gave you the painting—surely that is enough?'

'I have not given it to her yet. I realised she would insist on thanking you personally. If you recall, before you shoved the painting in my hands I had offered you a very good deal to refuse all contact with her—which you turned down spectacularly.'

Lucy couldn't believe her momentary loss of temper had led to this. 'What if I change my mind and agree now?' she asked.

'Too late, Lucy. The circumstances have changed. Thanks to Teresa Lanza, the August edition of a popular Verona society magazine has a full-page spread of her nephew's wedding—including pictures of you and I and an article about our tragically linked family histories. The so-called accident being once again in the press necessitates a change of plan. You and I will visit my mother as a couple, and you will present the painting to her as a personal gift. She will be delighted, and any speculation on the accident will fade away. Then, after a suitable period, when I tell my mother we are no longer an item she will understand the reason for no further contact and we need never meet again. In return Steadman's will be yours, and as for the rest I'll find you another partner.'

She looked up at him with horrified eyes. 'You can't possibly mean what I think you mean.'

'To qualify—I mean a partner in the building development,' he drawled sardonically, and she saw the way he was looking at her, his eyes running over her in an insolent masculine fashion that insulted rather than approved. 'I am well aware you are more than capable of finding another sexual partner, but for as long as you are with me I insist on exclusivity. Don't worry, it is not a long-term commitment. I have never kept a woman I liked for more than six months. With a woman like you it will probably be a lot less, and you will be free and clear.'

'You really are a first-class despicable bastard.' Her eyes flashed her contempt at him. 'You must be out of your tiny mind to think for a second I'd agree to such a proposition.'

Lorenzo shrugged. 'Take it or leave it,' he said, his hands dropping from her waist. 'I can stand the heat. I doubt if you can. But if you don't mind going bankrupt and losing everything, do what you like.' He glanced around the room. 'This is a nice set-up you have here, and I doubt your artist friends will be happy to see it close.'

Lucy was free, but frozen to the spot. 'You can't possibly do that.'

'Yes, I can. I can close the factory, for a start. I'm a wealthy man, and its monetary loss is negligible to me. And every attempt you make to move on with the housing development I can block for as long as I choose—certainly long enough to see you go broke. Lucky for you,' he drawled mockingly, 'I choose to have you in my bed.'

Colour ran up her neck and face, and her eyes sparked with frustrated rage. But he was right, damn him. Lorenzo was a powerful banker with contacts all over the world. He could pull any strings he liked and make strong men quake. What chance did she have against him? Virtually none...

She looked at him with hatred, and yet she knew deep

down she was going to accept his offer. The factory, the development plan—all that she worked for—was out of her hands. He could wreck everything—even cause her to lose her home, her gallery and the friends that were her life…a life she loved…

'So what's it to be, Lucy? As if I need to ask.' His sardonic eyes took in her small taut figure with mocking amusement. 'You know you are going to agree.'

'Yes, but first I want a binding contract with—'

'Oh, no,' he cut in. 'This is strictly between you and I, and—as you once so memorably said—you will have to take me on trust. But we can shake on it in the English way.' And he held out his hand.

She looked at his strong tanned hand, the long elegant fingers, and then up at his hard, expressionless face. She had the strangest notion he was not as sure of himself as he appeared. She lowered her eyes, her lashes sweeping her pale cheeks, and called herself a fool for trying to read more into his offer than what it was—sex for money, but on a large scale—and reluctantly placed her hand in his.

'So polite, so prim, so British,' he mocked as his hand tightened around hers, pulling her closer. She tried to pull away but he wrapped her hand behind her back, jerking her hard against him. 'That's better,' he said, his free hand unfastening the buttons of her shirt.

'Why are you doing this?' she asked helplessly. The brush of his fingers in the valley of her breasts as he deftly opened her shirt aroused a pulsating sensation deep inside her that she fought to control. 'I won't enjoy it, and you will get no pleasure from me.'

'Oh, I will, Lucy.'

He stared down at her, reading her reaction as he trailed long fingers over the curve of her breasts, dipping beneath the lace of her bra to graze a nipple. She gasped.

'You see, sweetheart?' He mocked her with the endearment as he teased a taut nipple between his long fingers. 'Your pleasure is my pleasure.' His mouth lowered to hers. The burning pressure of his kiss ignited her fiercely controlled feelings and she trembled helplessly. 'I am *so* going to pleasure you, Lucy,' he murmured against her mouth. 'What we had before will seem like a mere taste, and you will be begging me for more.'

'Never!' she cried, but her body seemed to have a will of its own, and she had a terrible desire to touch him, to surrender herself to the sweet agony of his kiss, his caress...

He slipped the shirt from her shoulder along with her bra strap, so he could bend his head to kiss the curve of her neck. She swayed, whimpering in protest, but as he lowered his head further, peeling down her bra to tongue her hardening nipples, the whimper changed to a moan of pleasure.

He lifted his head and she stared up at him, her eyes fixed on his hard, irresistible mouth.

'Still think you won't enjoy it?' he prompted and, dropping his hand, he removed her shirt and bra completely. His black eyes flicked over her from her pink lips, swollen from his kisses, over her slender shoulders to her breasts and the pale rose nipples betraying her arousal. 'Your body is telling me otherwise.'

Naked to the waist, and shamed by her own weakness, Lucy made an attempt to fold her arms in front of her. But he caught her hands and held them at her sides, bent his head, his mouth finding hers again.

The slow, seductive pressure of the kiss coaxing her lips apart was irresistible, and she could feel herself weakening, responding, wanting him—and suddenly she was transported back to the first time they'd made love…the heady excitement…the swirling senses…the exquisite delight of his touch.

Without removing his lips from hers, he swung her up in his arms. With a sense of *déjà vu* she grasped his shoulder, her hand curving around his neck to touch his hair. Her tongue was curling with his, and any lingering thought of resistance was swept away by the flood of desire raging through her.

He carried her into the bedroom and lowered her on to the bed, removing her shorts and briefs in one deft movement. He straightened up, staring down at her with hot hard eyes as he shed his clothes, letting them fall in a heap on the floor.

Lucy did not move. She was mesmerised at the sight of him. It was still daylight outside, and every muscle, every sinew of his great body was perfectly defined. But his facial muscles were tense, his strong jaw clenched as if to control some strong reaction. She had no time to wonder why as he joined her on the bed. The press of his hard body against her, the heat and the strength of him, made her tremble. Leaning over her, he brushed his lips against her brow, the curve of her cheek, and finally her mouth, to kiss her with an oddly gentle passion that was utterly beguiling.

He moved and laid his head against her breasts, turning his face to nuzzle their creamy fullness, suckling and licking the pouting tips as his hands stroked and caressed the quivering flesh down her hips, her thighs, and between her trembling legs. Every nerve in her body was screaming with tension almost to breaking point. Perspiration broke out on her brow, her body, and her small hands clutched at his biceps, his shoulders, roaming restlessly.

Suddenly Lorenzo rolled over onto his back, lifting her over him, his strong hands grasping the top of her legs. With one mighty thrust he impaled her on the rock-hard length of him, and stilled.

'I want to watch you fall apart,' he grated.

Eyes wild, she looked down and saw the molten passion in the black depths of his.

She splayed her hands on his chest and tried to move, his thickness filling her. She needed to move. But a finger slid between the velvet lips where their bodies joined and her head fell back, a long groan escaping her as he delicately massaged the swelling point of pleasure until she shattered into a million pieces. His grip tightened, holding her firm as she convulsed around him in a mind-blowing orgasm.

Only then did he move his hand to her waist and lift her. Rocking his pelvis, he plunged up deeper into her, over and over again, holding her fast until her shaking body trembled on the brink again. Then he spun her beneath him and his mouth covered hers, catching her desperate whimpering moans before he thrust into her with one fierce lunge that seemed to touch her womb and his great body joined hers in a shuddering climax that went on and on in mindless ecstasy.

Lucy fought for breath her internal muscles still quivering in the aftermath of release, her heart pounding. She was conscious of the heavy beat of Lorenzo's heart against her chest as he lay sprawled across her, his head buried in the pillow over her shoulder. How long she lay in mindless awe at what had happened she had no idea, but finally she lifted an arm to wrap it around him, then stopped and let it fall back on the bed.

In contrast to her body, hot and wet with sweat, her heart was suddenly as cold as ice. This was lust, not love, and she must never forget that… Last time when they had made love— There she was, doing it again… When they had had sex, she amended, Lorenzo had disillusioned her so brutally she had felt ashamed, cheap and dirty…

Well, not any more… It was way past time she toughened up—forgot about love and marriage and being the hopeless romantic Lorenzo had called her at Samantha's wedding. Equality of the sexes and all that—not that she had seen much of it so far in her life. But if Lorenzo could enjoy sex for sex's sake then so could she. Her morals were still intact—just in abeyance for a while. The fact that he had none wasn't her problem. And if it suited the swine to pay for the pleasure, then let him.

Ever the fatalist, she knew she'd have to be an idiot to turn down the deal he was offering. Anyway, she didn't have a choice—unless she wrecked a host of other people's lives, and that she could not do. On the plus side, she had no doubt he would soon tire of her, and then she could forget he'd ever existed and get on with her life the way she wanted to.

'I'm too heavy for you, and I need the bathroom,' Lorenzo said practically, and disappeared into the bathroom. Of course he never forgot protection—which was good in the circumstances. But then a man like Lorenzo—powerful and a control freak—had had plenty of practice…

He practised a lot more when he came back to join her on the bed, and when he finally slid off the bed and dressed he stared down at her for a moment. 'Sort out tomorrow when you can take three days off—preferably within the coming month.'

'I can't possibly. I have a business to run...'

'Yes, you can. Your friends will be out of work if you don't.'

'Only Elaine works for me, and she can't run the place on her own. Sid and Leon just display their work here, and I get ten percent of their sales.'

'Ten?' He shook his head. 'It should be much more than that.' And, bending over her, he dropped a kiss on her nose, a sensual gleam in his dark eyes. 'You have many good points, Lucy, that I am well acquainted with.' He smiled. 'But at the risk of sounding repetitive, trust me—business really isn't one of them.' He chuckled, and left.

Lucy lay where he'd left her. She knew she should be furious—and she would be later—but right at this moment all she felt was a languorous sense of physical satisfaction, and she fell into a deep sleep.

# CHAPTER SEVEN

THE tourist trade fell off as children returned to school. The summer was virtually over and Lucy was in a plane flying to Italy, trying to come to grips with the course her life had taken. It wasn't easy. She looked out of the window and below her could see the snow-covered peaks of the Alps, sparkling in the sun. Their beauty was lost on her. She was, for want of a better description, Lorenzo's mistress. She had become accustomed to travelling in a chauffeured car and a private jet...how bizarre was that...?

Lorenzo, after that fatal night when he had given her no choice but to become his lover, had virtually taken over her life, and the following morning had charmed Elaine into believing he was genuinely interested in Lucy. Obviously she could not deny it, and it had left her playing the part of his girlfriend all day, every day. The strain was beginning to tell.

That first day Lorenzo had whisked her away for dinner at the luxury country house hotel he had stayed at before, and the pattern had been set. Sometimes he would arrive and take her to the hotel—other times he'd send a car to take her to Newquay or Exeter Airport and the short flight to London, where Lorenzo kept a hotel suite when he was working in the city—which he had been doing a lot lately. Though now she had not seen him for five days—the longest they had been apart. Maybe it was not coincidence. He had stipulated at the beginning that she was to visit Italy in a month. It was exactly a month today. She had a growing feeling this visit would be the conclusion of their relationship. He had got what he wanted. As for Lucy, she was not sure what *she* wanted any more...

Lorenzo was a highly-sexed man, and they rarely got further than the bed—though a desk and the shower and on one memorable occasion a chair outside on the balcony had all figured in their sex-life.

Yet Lucy knew him little better now than she had the first time they'd met. He was for the most part a reserved, emotionless man, who gave little away except in the bedroom, where sometimes, with his dry wit and humour, he made her laugh. Other times he could be incredibly tender, and kiss and caress her as though he adored her. He always called her to arrange their meetings, but occasionally he called just to talk, and she could almost believe they were a normal couple. But maybe that was just wishful thinking on her part. Alone in her own bed at night, aching for him deep down, she knew for her it was more than just sex.

One thing she had learned about him and liked best was that he wore gold-rimmed glasses when working. Somehow they made him look younger and even more attractive, softening his hard face.

Well, maybe not *best*—because she could not deny the sex was fantastic. He had, with skill and eroticism, taught her more about the sensual side of her nature than she had imagined possible. She no longer made any attempt to resist, but welcomed him with open arms, and she knew when it was over between them there would be no other man for her. She could not imagine doing with any man what she did with Lorenzo...didn't want to...

The flight attendant—a handsome young man about her age—appeared, and offered to fasten her seat belt as they were about to begin their descent to the airport. She refused and fastened it herself, because there was something about the way he looked at her she didn't like. But then he was probably accustomed to ferrying women around the world to meet up with his boss, so she could hardly blame him for thinking the worst.

Lucy walked down the steps from the plane, blinking in the bright light, and smoothed the skirt of the red suit she wore down over her hips. A suit Lorenzo had bought for her the one day he had taken her out for lunch in London on what could pass for a date. Afterwards he had insisted on taking her shopping in Bond Street. She had tried to refuse, but he'd reminded her he was the boss and he wanted to see her in fine clothes and lingerie.

She looked up to see Lorenzo striding towards her, as immaculately dressed as ever in a grey suit, his hair as black as a raven's wing gleaming in the midday sun. Her heart turned over. He stopped in front of her and she glanced up through the thick fringe of her lashes, suddenly feeling too warm.

'Good—you made it,' he said coolly and, taking her arm, added, 'This is a private airfield and Customs are a mere formality.' He led her across the tarmac.

No greeting or kiss, Lucy noted. But then sadly they did not have that kind of relationship.

Ten minutes later she was sitting in the back of another chauffeured car, her nerves jangling as Lorenzo slid in beside her, his muscular thigh lightly brushing hers. She could sense the tension mounting in the close confines of the car as the silence lengthened, and finally found her voice. 'How long does it take to get to Lake Garda?'

He turned his head, his dark eyes meeting hers. 'We are going to my apartment in Verona first.'

Lifting a hand, he swept a tendril of hair that had escaped from her severely styled chignon behind her ear, and she felt the touch of his fingers down to her toes, a flush of heat staining her cheeks.

'I think you need to relax before travelling further. I know *I* do,' he said with a predatory smile that left her in no doubt as to what he had in mind.

To her shame, she felt an immediate physical response. Hastily she looked away, and heard him chuckle.

Lorenzo's apartment was a shock. Lucy stood in the huge living room, eyes wide in surprise. She had expected something formal—and it was. Elegant blue and cream drapes hung at the tall windows of the main reception room, and two huge blue silk-covered sofas flanked a white-veined marble fireplace. The bookshelves either side were stuffed with books—hardback and paperback, shoved in haphazardly—and in front stood a big leather captain chair in *scarlet!* A large low glass table had papers and magazines scattered all over it. The room was a bit of a mess...

But a fabulously expensive mess, she realised. An antique bureau had a bronze statue of a naked lady—pure Art Deco—standing on it, along with an incredible yellow and blue glass sculpture of a fish and a carved wooden statue of what looked like a Native American Indian. But it was the walls that really captured her attention. She recognised a Picasso from his Blue Period, a Matisse, and what she was sure was a Gauguin, along with some delicate watercolours and a huge Jackson Pollock that almost filled one wall.

She turned to Lorenzo and saw he had shed his jacket and had tugged his tie loose so the knot fell low on his chest. 'This is nothing like I imagined.' She waved her hand around, grinning delightedly.

'I know it looks a bit untidy, but Diego, my houseman, is on holiday, and I am not in the least domesticated,' he said wryly.

'I had noticed,' Lucy quipped, recalling the way he stripped off and dropped his ruinously expensive clothes anywhere, without a second thought, every time they met. 'But what I meant was I *love* the room—it is so colourful, and the art work is incredible. Some of it I would never have expected you to like.'

He reached for her then, his dark eyes holding hers and his hands closing over her shoulders 'Not quite such a staid old banker as you thought?' he queried, his hands slipping beneath the lapels of her jacket to peel it off her shoulders and drop it on the back of the sofa.

'I never think of you as old,' Lucy murmured, and the tension between them thickened the air as a different silent conversation took place. She was braless, and the white camisole she wore suddenly felt like a straitjacket.

He glanced down at her breasts, knowing he would see her nipples jutting against the silk. He raised his eyes, reaching for her hair and pulling out the pins. 'I love…your hair.' He ran his long fingers through the silken length. 'The colour is incredible—tawny like a lion is as near as I can get,' he murmured, and closed his arms around her. His dark head bent and the smouldering flame of desire glittered in his eyes as he touched his mouth gently against hers.

It was what Lucy had been waiting for from the moment she had stepped off the plane, if she was honest. The moment she'd set eyes on him he had excited her like no other man ever had or ever would. One look, one touch, and she wanted him—craved him with an intensity of emotion she could not deny. And the more she saw him the worse it got. He filled her every sense until nothing else existed but the consuming need to feel him take her to that magical place where for a few incredible moments they became one explosive entity. However much she tried to pretend it was just sex, deep down she knew she had fallen in love with Lorenzo.

His mouth was like silk, his tongue teasing and easing between her eagerly parted lips, but the gentleness swiftly gave way to a kiss of mutual desperate passion. His hands reached down to the hem of her skirt and tugged it up over her hips. Lucy grasped his shoulders as she felt his long fingers slip between her thighs and rip the lace briefs from her body and she didn't care. She was lost to everything but her hunger, her need for him.

He lifted his head, his face flushed and his black eyes holding hers as he zipped open his pants. 'I want you now,' he grated, and found her mouth again.

Lucy met and matched his demand instantly, totally, pushing her hands beneath his shirt, digging her fingers into the muscles of his back as he gripped her hips and lifted her. Wantonly she gave herself up to the fierce desire driving her, locking her legs around him. His tongue stoked deeper into her mouth and she cried out as he thrust up into the slick, heated centre of her.

The incredible tension tightened as he stretched her, filled her with deep plunging strokes, twisting, thrusting faster, building into an incredible climax that sent her mindless into a shuddering, shimmering wave of endless satisfaction. Then against her mouth Lorenzo groaned her name as he plunged one last time, his heart pounding out of control against hers, his great body shaking.

The silence afterwards was not restful but strained, Lucy slowly realised, shakily dropping her legs from his body, letting her hands fall from his shoulders. He stepped back and zipped up his trousers, and she smoothed her skirt down over her hips. She spied her ripped briefs on the floor. She glanced up at Lorenzo. He was watching her, and had seen the direction of her gaze. Then he spoke.

'Your briefs are finished, Lucy, and your luggage has already gone on to the house. You will have to go commando for a while—but that is probably nothing new for you,' he said with the arch of a brow, before adding, 'I could use a coffee—how about you?'

Lucy nodded her head. 'Yes,' she murmured, and he turned and disappeared through the door to the hall. His 'commando' comment told her everything she needed to know. He had no respect for her at all...never had and never would...

She spotted a few pins on the floor and, picking them up, clipped back her hair. She took her jacket off the back of the sofa and slipped it on, fastened it with a slightly unsteady hand. She was still wearing her high-heeled sandals, and wished viciously she had stabbed him in the back with them five minutes ago.

Still trembling inside, she walked across to the window and looked down at the street below, drawing in a few deep, calming breaths. A steady flow of cars drove along the road, and the pavements were full of people of all ages—some single, some couples and families—all chattering and laughing, going about their daily life as she'd used to do.

So what had happened to her? Lorenzo had happened, and she didn't know herself any more. Worse, she no longer liked herself. She had become one of those weak-willed women she normally pitied—a slave to her senses because of a man. In that moment Lucy knew she could not go on like this. She straightened her slender shoulders and folded her arms across her body, her mind made up. When this visit was over, so was her relationship with Lorenzo—whether he liked it or not. He could do his damnedest, but to save herself she could no longer afford to care.

In trying to be responsible and help other people she had given in to what amounted to blackmail. If she was brutally honest she had not fought very hard to avoid it, and in the process had lost all her self-respect.

She should have known from the start. She had tried before to be responsible for another, to help Damien, and it had ended in tragedy anyway. If Steadman's closed and the development never took place, so be it—at least the town had the seven acres of land she had donated. As for the family home, she would do as the estate agent had suggested weeks ago, when he'd told her that after twelve years of neglect the house badly needed updating and with the smaller garden the best option now was to put it up for auction and sell it for whatever she could get in the current market. She would, and then hopefully she could keep the gallery—probably still mortgaged, but at least she would own it.

'Coffee's ready.'

She turned around. Lorenzo was placing a tray on the glass table and trying to nudge papers out of the way. He sank down on the sofa and, picking up the coffee pot, filled two cups, then glanced across at her. 'Do you take milk and sugar?'

He didn't even know that much about her, she thought bitterly, and it simply reinforced her decision to end things.

'No, thanks. I need the bathroom—where is it?'

'There is one off my bedroom—I'll follow you through. Coffee in bed quite appeals,' he said, with a smile that was a blatant invitation.

'Not to me, it doesn't,' Lucy said coolly. 'Just tell me where the bathroom is. After all, I am here to visit your mother, and it is bad manners to keep her waiting.' She saw the flash of surprise in his eyes and watched them narrow, and felt a chill go through her.

Lorenzo was not accustomed to being denied, and his expression hardened as he looked at Lucy. She had pinned back her hair, replaced her jacket and fastened it, and was now standing stiffly, her arms folded in front of her, defiance in every line of her seductive body. He could make her do as he wanted—but suddenly he no longer had the stomach for it.

'In the hall—second on the left.' He gestured with his hand at the door he had just come through. Lucy was right. It was time they left.

He had shocked himself earlier, taking her without a second thought over the back of the sofa, totally out of control. This could not go on. The ice-cold anger and rage that had consumed him when he'd discovered Lucy had done a deal behind his back had cooled down, and he wasn't proud of the way he had behaved.

With the benefit of hindsight he should have agreed with Lucy the day she'd come to his office—agreed to support the status quo, leaving the running of Steadman's in the hands of the employee who had been dealing with it for the last five years. Instead he had let his anger over his brother's death be stirred up by his lunch with

Manuel and reacted badly. He had made his decision in anger instead of with his usual cool control. And getting involved with Lucy was another crazy mistake. In fact, he realised most of the summer had been one of crazy decisions on his part.

He was a normal, intelligent, healthy man, who enjoyed an active sex-life, but with Lucy he was in danger of allowing sex to take over his life to the detriment of his work and his leisure. He could not allow it to continue.

Since the day he had met her he had slept only one single night at his villa in Santa Margherita and only half a day sailing. And it was well over a month since he had been to New York. Instead he had spent most of his time in England, flying back and forth from Italy, and it had to stop. He still lusted after Lucy, but that was all it was—lust. Without conceit he knew that with his power and wealth he could take his pick of women, and occasionally had in the past. He would again.

His decision made, he rose to his feet and buttoned his shirt. The solution was simple: he just needed to get through the next three days, finish things with Lucy, then move on to a woman more his type who would not disturb the smooth running of his life.

His picked his jacket off the floor and slipped it on, then tightened his tie. When Lucy reappeared he moved towards her. 'Ready to go?'

Lucy glanced at him. 'Yes,' she said, equally direct.

Taking her elbow, he ushered her out of the apartment and down onto the street. 'Get in,' Lorenzo said, holding open the passenger door of a low-slung, lethal-looking yellow sports car.

Lucy did, and quickly fastened the seat belt. She didn't feel safe in this monster of a car, even when it was stationary. She glanced at Lorenzo as he slid into the driving seat and was about to ask what make the car was. But one look at the determined set of his jaw made her change her mind.

There was no other way to describe it—the man drove as if he had a death wish, Lucy thought. The countryside flashed past them in a whirl, and she caught her breath as the car swung around corners.

'Do you *have* to drive so fast?' she finally demanded.

He cast her a sidelong glance and said nothing, but she noticed he did slow down a little, and she could breathe easily again.

Her first glance of Lake Garda made her catch her breath again, and as Lorenzo drove along the one road that ran around the lake she was captivated by the small villages they passed. Eventually he guided the car between two stone towers that supported massive iron gates. The drive wound steeply up through a forest of trees and then veered right. Suddenly the forest ended, and Lucy simply stared in awe at the view before her.

The house was built in pale stone, beautifully proportioned, with circular turrets on all corners and with the forest as a backdrop. The gardens swooped down in lawns and terraces to the edge of the lake, where a wooden boat house was just visible by the trees. A small boat with its sails furled was tied up at the jetty. The overall view was idyllic, and incredible to her artistic eye. Someone had planned the garden skilfully. A pergola, a summerhouse and fountains were all strategically placed to draw the eye to a perfect flow of colour and symmetry.

'Lucy?'

It was the first word Lorenzo had spoken since they'd left Verona, and she glanced at her wristwatch. Well over an hour ago. She realised he had stopped the car. She looked out of the window, her eyes widening in admiration on the portico, a graceful structure with elegant arches and roof supported by four columns.

'Before we go in, a word of warning.'

She turned her head and looked at him. 'What? No stealing the silver?' she quipped.

He didn't so much as smile, just gave her a sardonic glance. 'That is an example of what I am afraid of. You are too impulsive, Lucy—you say everything that enters your head without a second thought.'

Not everything, Lucy thought. Even locked in his arms, in the throes of passion, she resisted the impulse to tell him she loved him.

'When you meet my mother you will be friendly and polite—no going over the top with hugs or confidences. I have the painting in the boot of the car. You will give it to her as a gift and she will be delighted. As for you and I—as far as my mother and the staff are concerned we will behave as close friends, though obviously we will not share a room. It is enough that I have brought you to the family home. Not something I ever do with the women in my life. That, along with an occasional arm around you, will confirm my mother's opinion—thanks to the Lanza woman—that we are a couple. When I tell her it is over between us you will have an excellent reason for no further contact that she will readily accept. Understand?'

'Perfectly. Machiavelli could not have come up with a better plan.'

The arrogance of the man confounded her. When he dumped her she was supposedly going to be so broken-hearted she would cut off all contact with the Zanelli family. The sad thing was she realised he was probably right—though he did not know it.

Forcing a smile to her face, she added, 'You mean pretend we are lovers but no mention of casual sex? I get it.'

'Lucy, cut out the flippant remarks. This is very straightforward. All you have to do is behave yourself in a restrained manner for a couple of days.'

'Yes, I see.'

And she *did* see—all too clearly. It was in his dark, impersonal eyes, in the hard face. He could not have made it clearer that when this visit was over so was she, as far as he was concerned. She turned her head away. It was what she wanted—to be free of him, she told herself, and tried to open the car door.

Before she could, it was swung open by a man Lorenzo introduced as Gianni—the butler!

Lucy stood in the grand hall, two storeys high, with a central staircase that split into two halfway up and ended in a circular balcony. Her green eyes fixed on the lady descending the marble stairs.

His mother was nothing like she'd expected, and when Lorenzo introduced her unexpectedly Lucy was hugged and kissed on both cheeks by the elegant woman. Lorenzo should have warned his mother not to go over the top, she thought. She'd been led to believe she was a frail little woman, but nothing could be further from the truth. Anna, as she insisted Lucy call her, was about five feet six, with thick curling white hair and sparkling brown eyes, and looked a heck of a lot fitter than Lucy felt.

Fifteen minutes later Lucy sat on a satin-covered chair in the most beautifully furnished room she had ever seen, with a glass of champagne in her hand, listening to Anna thanking her for what felt like the hundredth time for the portrait of Antonio.

She had always known Lorenzo was wealthy, but this house was more like a palace—and it seemed it was staffed like one. The butler had reappeared five minutes after they'd entered the room with the painting—gift-wrapped, Lucy had noted, probably down to Lorenzo.

She cast him a glance. He was lounging back on an exquisite antique gilt wooden-edged pink satin sofa, and he gave her the briefest of smiles that did not reach his eyes. If that was his idea of what would pass for 'close friendship' then heaven help him, she thought sadly.

The butler had appeared once more with the champagne, and a maid with a plate of tiny cakes.

To say his mother was ecstatic with her gift was an understatement. 'I can't thank you enough, Lucy.' Anna smiled across at her. The painting was now propped on top of the magnificent fireplace, half covering a picture of a stern-looking gentleman who looked remarkably like an older version of Lorenzo. 'You have captured my Antonio perfectly—but you knew him, and must have lots of photographs from the past. When did you paint it?'

'Well, it was in the March of my second year at college. Antonio and Damien had just come back from their round-the-world tour, and they were staying in the house I shared in London with two other students while they planned their mountaineering trip. I needed a model for a portrait as part of my end-of-year exam, and Antonio offered. Mind you, I had to bribe him to sit still with a constant supply of chocolate-covered Turkish delight, which he adored. Actually, it was good fun,' she said, smiling reminiscently. 'Though now I am older and more experienced I could probably do better.'

'Oh, no!' Anna declared. 'It is beautiful the way it is. It never occurred to me that Antonio had actually sat for you, but of course I can see it now. How else could you have caught him in that perfect moment in time, when he was at his best—healthy, happy and with friends? It is in his eyes, his smile, and it makes your gift doubly precious to me.'

'I'm glad you like it,' Lucy said inadequately, noting the shimmer of tears in Anna's eyes.

'I love it. And now a toast to my Antonio.' She raised her glass.

Lucy lifted hers to her mouth but only wet her lips. The little cake she had eaten had been sickly sweet, and what she could really do with was a cup of tea and something else to eat.

She looked at Lorenzo. He had drained his glass and was looking at his mother with such care and tenderness in his eyes it made her ache. He had never looked at *her* like that, and never would. She tore her gaze away and replaced her glass on the table, shifting restlessly in her chair.

'Champagne not to your taste, Lucy?' Lorenzo queried politely.

She glanced back at him. He was frowning at her—no tenderness in his eyes now, just black ice. She realised if she didn't get out of there soon she was going to scream—definitely not on Lorenzo's list of acceptable behaviour during the visit.

She was sitting there minus her briefs, needing to go to the bathroom, with a nice woman almost in tears and a man who hated her.

'Yes, it is fine,' she said, her green eyes filling with mockery. 'But if you will both excuse me?' She stood up. 'I have been travelling since eight this morning, and I would like to go and freshen up, please.'

'Of course, my dear. Where are my manners? I was so overcome...'

'Hush, Mother.' Lorenzo rose to his feet. 'I'll show Lucy to her room.' And, slipping an arm around her waist, he led her to the door. His mother smiled on benignly.

As soon as they were in the hall Lucy shrugged out of his hold. 'No audience now,' she sniped.

Lorenzo raised an eyebrow and said, 'Follow me.'

She did—up the elegant staircase to where Lorenzo turned right around the galleried landing to the front of the house, then along a corridor. He opened the second door on the left.

'My mother has the master suite next door, so you will be perfectly safe.'

Safe from what or who? Lucy wondered, and followed Lorenzo into the room. She gasped. The décor was all ivory and gold—the bed covered in the finest ivory satin and lace. Next to the fireplace was a *chaise-longue,* and a beautiful occasional table inlaid with hand-painted roses and humming birds. The whole effect was very feminine.

'The bathroom and dressing room are through there.' Lorenzo indicated a door at the opposite end. 'I believe the maid has unpacked your clothes. If there is anything else you need you have only to ring.'

She actually felt like wringing his neck. He was standing there so cool, so remote, when only hours ago he'd been ripping off her briefs. No—best not to go there...

'What I really need is a cup of tea and a sandwich.

Apart from that tiny cake I've had nothing to eat since I left home this morning, and I'm starving.'

'Surely you were offered lunch on the flight? It was all arranged.'

'I *was* offered lunch, but I refused because I got the impression the dashing young flight attendant was offering more.'

'What?' The polite mask had slipped to one of outrage. 'You should have told me—I will dismiss him immediately.'

'No—not on my account. His attitude is not surprising, really. He is probably used to flying loose women out to wherever you happen to be,' she said scathingly, and saw his jaw tighten, a flash of anger in his dark eyes.

Quickly stepping past him, she headed for the bathroom. She heard the bedroom door slam behind her and wasn't surprised.

# CHAPTER EIGHT

THE bathroom, like the rest of the house, was perfect. All pale marble, with a big raised bath and a very modern double shower. The vanity unit contained every possible bathroom accessory known to a man—and, she noted, her own modest toilet bag.

Spying a shower cap, she could not resist. She pulled it over her hair and picked up a top designer shower gel. Stripping off her clothes, she stepped into the shower and turned the water on, relishing the soothing spray as she used the heavenly scented gel to wash her body.

Finally she stepped out of the shower and, picking a large white towel off the pile stacked on a shelf, dried herself. Taking another one, she wrapped it sarong-style around her body. Then she took her hairbrush from her toilet bag and brushed her hair.

Lucy walked back into the bedroom feeling refreshed, and saw a tray holding tea and sandwiches on the table by the *chaise-longue*. Lorenzo had done as she'd asked, but she had no doubt the maid had delivered them. She flopped down on the *chaise-longue* and poured a cup of tea, then ate an Italian-style sandwich made with crusty bread and filled with cheese, tomato and something spicy Lucy didn't recognise. It was delicious.

\* \* \*

'Lucy? Lucy…'

Lorenzo didn't want to touch her—he was hard just looking at her. She was stretched out on the *chaise-longue* asleep, her hair tumbled over her shoulders and with one arm above her head, the other across her stomach. A towel that was wrapped around her had slipped to reveal one rose-tipped creamy breast. She was enough to tempt a saint. Yet in sleep, with her long lashes curled against her cheek, she had a look of innocence about her that twisted something inside him.

Slowly Lucy opened her eyes and yawned. She saw the tray with the tea and sandwiches, and realised she must have dozed off.

'Good—you are awake at last.'

At the sound of Lorenzo's voice she glanced up. He had changed into another suit, she noted—then she saw where his eyes rested and blushed scarlet. Quickly she sat up, pulling the towel over her chest.

He looked down at her, his dark eyes mocking. 'Nothing I have not seen before… But that is not what I came for. Dinner is at eight—you have half an hour to get ready. Before I go I should warn you my mother has arranged a party for Wednesday evening—she wants to introduce you to her friends. So you will not be able to leave until Thursday.'

'Well, you can just *un*arrange it,' Lucy said, knotting the towel firmly under her arm. She stood up, feeling vulnerable wearing just a towel when Lorenzo towered over her, his virile masculinity evident in every line of his long lean body, undisguised by the conventional dark suit he wore. With her temper and shamefully her pulse rising at the sight of him, she added, ' You will have to—because I told Elaine I would be back by

Wednesday night at the latest and she is taking Thursday morning off.'

'I knew nothing about the party until this evening. If I had I would have discouraged my mother. The whole point of this visit was to get you out of her life, not more involved.' Even as he said it Lorenzo realised it had been a crazy idea in the first place. What had he been thinking of? One glance at Lucy wearing a towel and he had his answer. She addled his brain without even trying, and the solution was to keep out of her way.

Lucy knew the purpose of this trip was to remove her from his mother's life, but it still stung to be reminded. Flashing him an angry glance, she saw the strong jaw clench as if to control some unwanted reaction, but a moment later she knew she had been mistaken.

'Anyway, it has nothing to do with me now,' he said with a negligent shrug of his broad shoulders. 'But do feel free to tell my mother to cancel.' A mocking smile curved his mouth. 'Rather you than me.'

Silently fuming, ten minutes later Lucy finally found her underwear, neatly packed away in drawers in the dressing room. She picked out a black dress from the few clothes she had brought with her, hanging forlornly in an enormous bank of empty wardrobes.

She had no time to fix up her hair, and had to be content with brushing it back behind her ears and fastening it with a silver slide at the nape of her neck. She used moisturiser on her face, and after a touch of mascara to her long lashes and an application of lipstick to her lips she slipped her feet into a pair of high-heeled sandals and was ready.

Finally she fastened a diamond-studded platinum watch on her wrist. It had been her mother's, and was her most treasured possession. She only wore it on special occasions. Though this wasn't a special occasion so much as a nightmare.

She had argued with Lorenzo that it was up to him to cancel the party, but he had shrugged her off. He had said it was up to her, as the party was basically for her benefit and if she insisted on going home on Wednesday, as planned, the party would not take place. He'd actually had the audacity to say that of course his mother would probably never speak to her again, which was a good result as far as he was concerned, and then walked out.

He knew damn fine, Lucy thought, walking down the grand staircase at a minute to eight, that it wasn't in her nature to be so appallingly bad-mannered. But then again maybe he *didn't* know—he thought she was little better than a street walker anyway.

She hesitated in the hall and adjusted the thin straps of the classic short black fitted dress she wore—another of Lorenzo's purchases. Her thinking was that she might as well wear them in his company, because once this charade was over they were going to a charity shop. She looked around. The walls were lined with what she guessed were family portraits, because the men all had a look of Lorenzo about them—though not quite as striking—and the women were all beautiful. Suddenly she didn't know what she was doing here, and was tempted to run back up the stairs.

But Gianni the butler appeared, and offered to escort her to the dining room. Smiling, she thanked him, her moment of panic over. Then her high heels slipped on the marble floor and she grabbed his arm, laughing with him as they entered the room, where Lorenzo and his mother were chatting quietly.

Both heads turned, and the butler quietly withdrew as Anna smiled and stepped forward. 'Lucy, I hope you are rested. I was so overcome by your gift I forgot you had been travelling all day and forgot my manners, I'm afraid,' she said disarmingly.

Lucy smiled. Anna was a delightful lady—a pity about her son, she thought, glancing at Lorenzo. He was lounging against the fireplace, a glass of what looked like whisky in his hand.

'Shall we sit down, ladies?' he suggested, straightening up and crossing to the long dining table perfectly set with silver and crystal. He pulled out a chair for his mother and Anna sat down. Then, crossing to the other side of the table, his dark eyes resting on her, he drawled softly, 'Lucy, *cara*. Be seated,' and gave her a smile, acting the perfect gentleman.

But Lucy knew otherwise, and realised immediately the endearment was for his mother's benefit. She returned his smile with a false one of her own and took the seat he offered.

After a rocky start, the dinner was not the ordeal Lucy had expected.

Anna insisted she try the red wine she'd had the butler open in her honour—an especially good one from a renowned Tuscan vineyard—and Lorenzo sat at the head of the table, with Lucy and his mother either side of him, which meant the two women could talk easily across the table.

The first thing Anna said, after the wine glasses were filled and the wine tasted, was, 'Lucy, dear, I know it was presumptuous of me to arrange a party for Wednesday evening, but I didn't realise your time was so limited and you were going home that day until Lorenzo told me earlier. He suggested it might be difficult for you to stay longer, as you have a business to run, but I do hope you can. All my friends are invited, and the Contessa della Scala is coming—she is really looking forward to seeing you again. Now, with the portrait, the party will be even better. You will make an old woman very happy, plus you and Lorenzo can spend more time together.' She beamed.

Emotional blackmail at its finest. Maybe it ran in the family? Lucy thought cynically. Lifting her chin, she looked at Lorenzo and caught the taunting gleam in his black eyes. She forced a slow smile to her lips. 'Your concern for my business is touching, Lorenzo, darling.' She baited him with an endearment of her own, and turned back to Anna as the first course was presented.

'Unfortunately my friend Elaine, who is taking care of the gallery, is expecting me back by Wednesday evening because she has a dental appointment on Thursday morning. But it is not an insurmountable problem. I can ring her tomorrow and tell her not to bother opening on Thursday. I can be back before Friday.'

'No, I would not think of putting you out that way,' Anna said immediately. 'Why should you lose business? Lorenzo can find someone to take care of your gallery for you, no trouble at all. In fact you could stay for the rest of the week. After visiting the dentist your friend would probably appreciate having the whole day off and more.'

Lucy had to bite her lip to stop herself laughing at the expression on Lorenzo's face as he looked at his mother in astonishment—horror quickly masked.

'You can do that, can't you, Lorenzo?' his mother queried.

Briefly he flicked Lucy a threatening glance, and

she knew he saw the amusement in her eyes before he looked back at Anna.

'Yes, of course I can, Mother—if Lucy agrees.' His gaze was on her again. 'I can probably arrange to get someone there by Wednesday afternoon, so Elaine can show them the ropes.' An eyebrow rose as he asked innocently, 'One day or two, Lucy?'

'One will be fine,' she said, knowing it was the answer he wanted. What was the point in defying him? She hadn't wanted to stay longer in the first place, so why prolong the agony? 'I must be home by Thursday night.'

'Good, then that is settled,' Anna said, and they finished their first course of risotto with red wine and porcini mushrooms.

The butler offered more wine and Lucy agreed, surprised to see she had finished the glass. But it was really nice, and very mellow.

Anna could certainly talk, Lucy thought as the plates were cleared by the maid. Mostly about Antonio—while Lorenzo sat looking on, his face a blank mask, adding very little to the conversation.

'According to the doctor Antonio was a miracle child. He was very ill when he was born, and it was touch and go for a while, but he made a complete recovery and was soon running all over the place like any other child. I did sometimes wonder if it was because I was a lot older when he was born that he had problems—it was ten years after I had Lorenzo. But he grew up to be a wonderful young man. I only wish I had kept him longer…'

It occurred to Lucy that if Anna had always been so loquacious about her youngest son it might go some way to explain why Lorenzo had grown into the hard, apparently emotionless man he was.

The conversation stopped as the main course was served—veal escalope Marsala—and Lucy tried to change the subject.

'You have a beautiful home, Anna. My bedroom is delightful, and the view from the window is lovely. I could not help noticing when I arrived that the gardens are magnificent, and so cleverly designed—whichever way one looks everything flows together perfectly. Someone at some time must have been a keen landscape gardener.'

'Gardening is my passion,' Anna said, obviously delighted by Lucy's interest. 'When Lorenzo started school my husband gave me permission to have the whole grounds redesigned. It was a huge project, and I spent three years deciding on and finding the flowers, the shrubs, the trees, the fountains—everything. Sometimes Lorenzo would come with me on my search for all the specimens I wanted. Mind you...' she looked lovingly at Lorenzo '...his taste ran to the most vibrant colours, which was odd given his serious nature.'

Lucy did not find it odd at all, having seen his apartment, but she could sense Lorenzo almost squirming in his chair, and cast him a sidelong glance. Not a muscle moved in his darkly attractive face, but when he noticed her looking he lifted a negligent brow and turned back to his mother.

'Lorenzo was a genius at mathematics at a very young age—my husband used to worry he might think he was too clever to settle for the role tradition demanded of him. But his skill was invaluable to me when it came to the design. He was only nine but he worked out all the angles, the lengths of the terraces and the paths where the fountains had to be placed for optimum effect, and made a complete plan for me. All the builder and gardeners had to do was the manual work.'

'That is amazing!' Lucy could not help exclaiming.

'Not really.' Lorenzo finally spoke. 'My mother is prone to exaggeration,' he said coolly, but tempered it with a smile.

The maid arrived and conversation ceased as the plates were cleared again. Dessert was brought in, and talk turned to the planned party.

Finally the butler suggested serving coffee, and Anna got to her feet and said, 'I never drink coffee at night, but you go ahead. I know you will be glad of some time on your own,' she prompted with a smile. 'I have had the most marvellous day I can remember in years, and I'm going to bed now.'

Lorenzo got to his feet to help her, but she refused and patted his cheek, so he bent to kiss hers and she left.

The silence was deafening.

'That went well,' Lorenzo finally said. 'My mother is happy and convinced we are close. Make sure you keep it that way until we leave on Thursday and everything you want is yours.'

Lucy looked up at him, her eyes tracing the hard bones of his face, the cool, steady eyes, the powerful jaw and mobile mouth. He had no idea what she really wanted, she thought sadly and, pushing back her chair, stood up.

'I will,' she said. 'Unlike you, I don't like deceiving your mother, and this can't be over quickly enough for me.' She turned towards the door, adding quietly, 'if you don't mind, I'll forgo the coffee.'

He moved quickly, his hand catching hers, and kissed

her palm. 'I don't mind anything you want, *cara*,' he husked, and her eyes widened in shock.

Her hand trembled in his grasp—and then she realised it was for the benefit of the butler, who had entered the room with the coffee tray. Pulling her hand free, she patted Lorenzo's cheek with more force than necessary and saw his lips tighten. 'You enjoy your coffee.'

Swiftly an arm closed around her waist, his dark head dipped, and he kissed her cheek, his warm breath caressing her ear. 'Not an option,' he murmured. 'Remember our deal? Everyone has to be convinced.' And, raising his head, he said, 'Take the coffee to the lounge, please, Gianni.'

Then his head bent again and his mouth closed possessively over hers, parting her lips. The prolonged assault on her senses swept away all her resistance. His hand moved sensually over her back to press her closer and she arched into him, her eyes closing in abandon.

Suddenly he lifted his head. 'Gianni has gone.'

Her eyes flew open as his comment registered. 'What did you do that for?'

'I saw the way Gianni looked at you, laughed with you when you entered the dining room with your body blatantly on display in that dress. He is a red-blooded man and he is not going to believe for a minute that holding your hand or a kiss on the cheek would satisfy me or any man. Now he will be convinced, and if he is the rest of the staff will be also.'

For a moment Lucy had the odd idea he was jealous of the butler. 'Does your brain ever stop working and planning your next move?'

'I've never really thought about it, but probably not—except perhaps in a moment of intense sexual relief,' he drawled, and ushered her out of the dining room and into the lounge, where the coffee was set on a low table in front of a sofa.

Lucy twisted out of his arm and sat down on the sofa, the colour in her face matching the pink satin, and leant forward to pour out a cup of coffee she did not want simply to hide her blush.

Lorenzo laughed and sat down beside her. 'You know, Lucy, for an experienced woman it never ceases to amaze me how easily you blush—how do you do it?'

She was tempted to tell him then how little experience she really had, but bit her lip and drank the coffee. He would never believe her. He had formed his opinion of her, coloured by his distorted perception of her brother and the ease with which she had fallen into bed with him the first time. By accepting his deal she had reinforced that low opinion, and nothing she could do would ever make him change his mind.

'Practice—just practice,' she said, telling Lorenzo what he wanted to hear.

'Did you practise with Antonio?' he asked. 'You have painted him with a happy smile on his face—did you sleep with him?'

Lucy's eyes widened to their fullest extent on his unsmiling countenance. He couldn't be serious, she thought. But he was, she realised—and suddenly she was furious.

Before she said something she knew she would regret, she got to her feet. 'No,' she said coldly. 'Unlike you, he was a gentleman. Now, if you are satisfied I have played my part as required, I am going to bed. And before you get up—don't bother. There is no one here to see you *playing* the gentleman.'

And she turned away and walked to the door,

leaving him to follow her or not…amazed by his cruel insensitivity…

She looked around the bedroom; someone had laid her nightdress on the bed and turned down the covers. Service at its best, she thought with a wry smile twisting her lips as she entered the bathroom, stripped off her clothes and put them away. She washed her face, cleaned her teeth and, naked, returned to the bedroom. Picking the nightdress off the bed, she slipped it over her head and crawled into the big bed.

She didn't expect to sleep, but surprisingly she did… She stirred once, at the tail-end of a dream of a shadowy figure of a man standing over her, but went straight back to sleep.

The next morning she awoke to the overpowering smell of strong coffee, and, easing herself up the bed, saw the maid approach with a tray which she placed on the bedside table.

'*Buongiorno, signorina*. The *Signora* say to bring coffee,' she said in fractured English, 'Breakfast in one hour.'

'*Grazie!*' Lucy said. '*Scusi—*' She sprang out of bed and dashed to the bathroom. When she returned, after having been sick, the maid was still there.

'*Signorina? Come stai?*'

Lucy saw the worried frown on her face and knew enough Italian to reassure her she was fine. The maid left.

It was probably the wine she'd drunk last night, Lucy thought. She was not accustomed to fine red wine—or any wine, for that matter. She poured out a cup of hot milk, with the merest dash of coffee, and standing looking out of the window sipped it slowly.

The view really was breathtaking… And then she

saw the yellow sports car shoot off down the drive. Good—Lorenzo had gone out. With no fear of him appearing, she relaxed a little.

She took a leisurely shower and wondered what to wear. It was a sunny day, and she wanted to have a look around the gardens. With that in mind she decided on a pair of soft denim jeans and bright flowing top. She tied her hair back in a ponytail and finally ventured out of the bedroom.

She did not need to look for the breakfast room. As soon as she reached the foot of the grand staircase Gianni appeared as if by magic and showed her to yet another room—not as large as the others she had seen, but just as elegant, and somehow more homely. Anna was already seated at the table, and looked up as she entered.

'How are you, Lucy? Maria told me you were a little unwell.' She frowned. 'Please sit down, my dear. My doctor calls to see me most days at noon—if you like you could see him as well.'

Lucy smiled and took a seat. 'No, that is not necessary. I am fine—just too much wine, I think,' she said with a rueful smile. 'But I wouldn't mind a walk in the gardens after breakfast. The fresh air will do me good.'

'Well, if you are sure, I will give you a guided tour,' Anna offered. 'Really it should be Lorenzo, but he has gone to the bank. I told him to take the day off, but he takes no notice of me. He works far too hard—always has. When my husband died—good man though he was—the bank was left in a poor condition. Lorenzo took over and soon put everything right, expanding all over the world, but sometimes I do wish he would slow down a little. Which is why I am so pleased he has found *you,* Lucy—you are just what he needs.'

'Oh, I wouldn't say that.' Lucy finally got a word in. 'We are close friends, but realistically we have very little in common.' And with a quick change of subject she added, 'Before I forget, I must call Elaine and tell her of the change of plan.'

Elaine was surprised but happy to agree to the new arrangement of taking Thursday off while the shop was looked after by a temp.

Lucy, on the other hand, was stressed to bits.

Oddly enough, once outside, with the scent of pine trees and perfumed flowers mingling in the warm morning air, Lucy felt better. Meandering with Anna along the paths and terraces of the glorious garden was relaxing. She learnt from Anna the names of dozens of plants, and when they got to the lake learnt the sailing boat had been Lorenzo's when he was a teenager, and he still used it occasionally.

According to Anna he was still a keen sailor, and spent most of his leisure time at Santa Margherita, where he had a villa. He kept a larger racing yacht at the marina, and sailed it very successfully in quite a few races round the Mediterranean.

Lucy was surprised. When Lorenzo had told her he had a yacht she had assumed he meant some big luxury motorised ship. A smile quirked her lips. She did think he looked like a pirate sometimes, so she should not be surprised, she told herself as they walked back to the house.

Lunch was served, and Anna's doctor, who was a widower, joined them at the table. He was a distinguished-looking, charming man, and Lucy warmed to him immediately. She had a sneaky suspicion his interest in Anna was more than medical...

Then the butler appeared, and Lucy was surprised when he informed her Lorenzo was on the private line and wishing to speak to her. He escorted her to the rear of the house, into what was obviously a study, and handed her the telephone.

'Hello?' she said. She could hear voices in the background, one a woman's—probably his secretary.

'Ah, at last.' Lorenzo's deep dark voice echoed in her ear. 'Are you getting along all right on your own, Lucy? No slip-ups?'

'Yes. And if by that you mean have I told your mother that her brilliant saintly son is really a rat? No, I have not.'

'Sarcasm does not become you. Do I detect a bit of frustration there? Missing me already?' he drawled throatily.

'Like a hole in the head,' she snapped, and heard him chuckle.

'No chance I would be given an opportunity to miss your smart mouth—you really know how to dent a man's ego.'

'Not yours, that's for sure.' Her pounding heart was telling her she was more disturbed by his flirtatious tone than she dared admit, but knowing it must be for his secretary's benefit she said, 'Cut the pretence and just tell me what you want. I am in the middle of lunch.'

'Right.' His voice was brusque. 'I have arranged with an English agency for a Miss Carr who lives in Cornwall to help at the gallery. She will call in tomorrow afternoon at three to arrange the details with Elaine. Tell my mother I have back-to-back meetings all day and

I'm staying in Verona tonight. I will be back tomorrow evening for the party. Can you do that?'

'Yes. If that is all, I am going back to finish my lunch.'

Lorenzo was deliberately staying away—or he might even have another woman lined up for tonight, Lucy thought. As if she needed any more proof it was over between them!

'Enjoy your meal,' he said, and hung up.

Lucy relayed the conversation when she got back to the table. Anna did not look happy, but accepted the news with grace.

# CHAPTER NINE

FOR some reason Lucy hadn't been able to enjoy her lunch—in fact she'd hardly eaten anything. The doctor, noticing, had mentioned that Anna had told him Lucy had been sick that morning and enquired if she still felt unwell.

Unthinkingly Lucy had told him she thought it was the red wine, because she didn't usually drink, and then added that she was not used to eating such rich food so late.

The doctor had agreed that might be true, but then mentioned the possibilities of gastro enteritis or food poisoning. Anna had looked mortified, and that was why Lucy was now lying on her bed, having submitted to numerous tests.

Lucy liked the elderly man, and at his enquiries had told the doctor about her medical history—including an operation she had undergone a few years earlier, which was one of the reasons she was careful what she ate and rarely drank, and probably why wine affected her so quickly. He had nodded his head and agreed with her.

Her lips twitched and parted in a grin, and she chuckled—then laughed out loud. She was the guest from hell...who had unwittingly implied her hostess had poisoned her. At least Lorenzo would be happy, because

when Lucy left there was not the slightest fear of Anna
wanting her to visit again.

On the contrary, Anna appeared to be quite happy when
Lucy went back downstairs. Dinner was arranged for
seven in Anna's favourite garden room at the side of the
house, where a small table was set for the two of them.
The meal was light and delicious, and Anna confessed
she usually ate there, only using the formal dining room
when Lorenzo was home—which Lucy gathered was
not very often.

Wednesday was chaotic. The huge house was a hive
of activity as caterers, florists and extra staff bustled
around the place.

The doctor came early—he was staying the night—
and after lunch, when Anna had retired to her room to
rest, told Lucy her blood tests were clear. It was probably, as she'd thought, the wine—or maybe the stress
of visiting Lorenzo's home and mother. He remembered
when he'd met his late wife's parents for the first time
he'd been sick with nerves before he even got to their
house.

Lucy tried to laugh, thanked him, and followed Anna
upstairs.

She had a leisurely soak in the huge bath before wash-
ing her hair, and then, not feeling in the least tired,
decided to go out into the garden and let her hair dry
naturally in the fresh air, as she did at home. She pulled
on jeans and a light blue sweater and, slipping her feet
into soft ballet shoes, she stuck a comb in her pocket
and left the house. There were so many people running
around she would not be missed.

It was another sunny afternoon, with a slight breeze

rustling the trees, and she wandered down the garden until the noise from the house faded away. Finally she stopped on one of the terraces. A circular fountain stood there, with water cascading down from a fifteen-feet-high centrepiece into a big pool, where koi carp in various shades of gold and yellow were swimming lazily around.

She sat down on a seat conveniently placed, and taking the comb from her pocket pulled it through her hair. It was half dry already. With a sigh she closed her eyes and turned her face up to the sun. Bliss, she told herself. Just one more day and then no more Lorenzo. She would have her life back. But the pain in her heart told her she lied.

'Lucy—I have been looking all over for you.'

For a second she thought she had conjured his voice up in her mind, then her eyes flew open. Lorenzo was standing a foot away, his dark gaze fixed on her face.

'What are you doing out here?'

'Nothing,' she muttered. He was wearing a suit, but his jacket and tie were loose, his black hair dishevelled, and he was looking grimly at her, as if she had committed a cardinal sin. Even so she felt herself tense in instinctive awareness of the magnetic attraction of his big body. 'I didn't realise I had to ask permission,' she said sarcastically, to hide her involuntary reaction to him.

'You don't. But I rang before lunch and spoke to my mother. She told me you were sick and you saw her doctor—are you all right?'

'You are a day late. That was yesterday, and I am fine.'

His apparent concern was too little, too late, and she wasn't fooled by it for a second. It was over. He had made that plain on Monday and they both recognised it—which was why she had not seen him since.

'I guess she told you I think it was the wine and the food. Sorry about that. But, hey—look on the bright side, Lorenzo. She must think I am the guest from hell, accusing her of poisoning me. She will *never* invite me back.'

He didn't so much as crack a smile. If anything, he looked even grimmer.

'No, she hinted you might be pregnant. Very clever, Lucy, but no way will you catch me in *that* trap.' His lips twisted in a sneer. 'If you are pregnant try your last partner—because it has nothing to do with me. I was meticulous with contraception, as you well know, *cara*.'

Only Lorenzo could make an endearment sound like an insult, Lucy thought sourly. If she had ever had the slightest glimmer of hope that he might care for her it was snuffed out in that moment.

Flushed and angry now, she rose to her feet. Tilting back her head, she let her green eyes mock him. 'I'm not pregnant, but thank you for that. It confirmed my sketch of you was spot-on.'

She turned to leave, but he caught her wrist.

His dark eyes flicked over her, from the striking mass of her hair to her pink lips and the curve of her breasts, making her wince at the mixture of contempt and desire she saw in his eyes as they finally met hers.

'This changes nothing. You will behave yourself to-night, stay silent on your brother and the accident, and I will put you on the plane myself tomorrow—is that understood?'

'Yes. Message well and truly received,' she said bit-terly, and all the anger and resentment she had bottled up for so long came pouring out. 'For your information, I loved my brother, and I believe he did his best on that mountain—unlike you, who would believe the worst of anyone without a second thought. Antonio said you were a ruthless bastard admiringly, almost with pride, but I bet he never realised you actually are. You hate my brother because of the accident. But Damien did what the experts and the coroner all agreed was the correct thing to do in the circumstances. He cut the rope to go and get help for Antonio and he succeeded. The fact that rescue was too late was nobody's fault—just fate...'

She paused for a moment, remembering. 'But that was not good enough for *you*. With your arrogance and superior intellect you decided they were all wrong. And you couldn't resist taking a bit of revenge out on me, because I'm Damien's sister.' She shook her head in disgust, her hair flying wildly around her shoulders. 'The irony of it is, if I was the one hanging over a cliff tied to you I'd bet my last cent you would cut the rope without hesitation. You make me *sick*,' she said contemptuously.

Lorenzo reached out and, catching her shoulders, jerked her forward, crushing her against him. Ruthlessly his mouth ground down on hers, and he kissed her with an angry passion that had nothing to do with love—only dominance. She struggled to push him away, but her hands were trapped between their bodies. And to her self-disgust even now she could sense herself weakening, responding. In a desperate effort of self-preservation she kicked out with her foot and caught his shinbone, and suddenly she was free.

If she had hurt him Lucy was glad. He deserved a hell of a lot more than a kick in the shin for what he had done to her.

'You are coming with me,' he said and, catching her

wrist, pulled her forward. 'As for cutting the rope—I would never tie myself to *you* in the first place,' he said scathingly, his eyes deadly. 'Cutting the rope is not why I despise your brother. It is because I have proof that he could have saved Antonio and chose not to.'

Lucy drew in a sharp breath. 'That is a horrible thing to say and I don't believe you,' she lashed back at him. 'Maybe it is your own guilty conscience looking for a scapegoat. According to Antonio you spent most of your time in America with a string of different women and he rarely saw you.'

'That's it,' he snarled. 'I will show you the evidence and that will be the end.' And he almost frogmarched her back to the house.

Oblivious to the surprised looks from the dozens of people in the hall, he marched her to the rear of the house, pushed open a door, and led her into the study.

'Sit,' he instructed, and shoved her onto a well-worn black leather sofa. He walked over to a large desk and, opening a drawer, withdrew something, then walked back to stand towering over her.

'You need proof of what an apology for a man your brother was?' He flung a handful of photographs down on the low table in front of her. 'These are pictures taken on the day of the so-called accident that killed Antonio. Look at them.'

He leant over and spread them out in front of her. The first he pointed to was of Antonio and Damien, their faces almost as red as the jackets they wore, laughing. Moisture glazed Lucy's eyes as she stared at the picture. They both looked so young, so vibrant, so full of life— and now they were both dead.

'That is the pair of them arriving at the base camp to

prepare for the climb the next morning. Note the date and time on all of them.'

Lucy didn't see the point. The date of the accident was imprinted on her mind for all time. But she did as he said. Three more were general shots the same day, and within the same hour. Only the fifth—a landscape shot—was of the following day, at two in the afternoon.

'So they look happy?' She brushed a tear from her eye. 'What am I supposed to see?'

'See the small figure in red on the landscape shot that is your brother. These photographs were given to me by a friend, Manuel, who is an expert climber. Damien and Antonio were not at his level, but were experienced climbers. They joined the climbing club together at university, climbed regularly in Britain, in the Alps, and on other continents when they toured the world.' He looked down at her, his black eyes blazing with anger. 'According to Manuel, from the position of your brother on the mountain at that time any reasonably experienced climber could have made it to the base camp in three hours—four at the very most. But it was dark when your brother called the rescue service—*seven hours* after that photograph was taken—too dark to start the search. A complete novice could have got down faster. He let Antonio die.'

Lucy looked up at him. For a second she thought she saw a glimmer of anguish in his eyes, and then it was gone, and he was watching her, waiting, supremely confident in his belief, his dark gaze challenging her to deny the evidence he was presenting her with.

Should she bother? Lucy asked herself. She knew Lorenzo. When he made up his mind about something nothing changed it. He was always right. He had decided she was a promiscuous woman the first time she went to bed with him for no other reason than that she had... He looked at a few photographs and decided they were proof her brother was a murderer, though he had not used that term...

'You really believe that?' Lucy said quietly.

'Yes—the proof is in front of you. Antonio is dead. I lost a brother, and Damien cost my mother her son and devastated her life.'

Lucy's eyes widened. She'd been devastated at Antonio's death, maybe, but Anna still had Lorenzo— her life was hardly over. And she was fed up with being the bad guy—or girl, in her case.

'It didn't do a lot for my life, either, or I would not be sitting here listening to this,' she said sarcastically. 'I have finally realised everything is black and white with you, Lorenzo. Good or bad—no in between. You are always right. Does it ever occur to you not everyone is as strong as you are? Perhaps after hanging onto Antonio for over an hour Damien was weak? Perhaps he passed out and didn't remember? Or maybe the clock was wrong?' she ended facetiously.

'No, there can be no other explanation, Lucy. The evidence is all there in the coroner's report. Your brother said he thought it had taken him four hours to reach the camp, not seven. The coroner's report states Antonio had died not of his injuries but of hypothermia, after spending the night on the mountain, only one or two hours before he was found. He could have lived if it wasn't for your damned brother. So now you have seen the proof, and now you know why Steadman is a dirty word to me.'

Lucy thought of arguing and looked at him. His face was set hard and she shivered. What was the point?

Lorenzo was a strong man—not the type to accept weakness in others.

'Have you nothing to say?' he asked, his dark gaze resting on her.

'Thank you for showing me the photos.' She stood up. 'Can I go now?'

Lorenzo watched her. Damn it, she looked like a schoolgirl in her flat shoes—but he knew she wasn't. Her head was slightly bowed, her beautiful face pale, her expressive eyes guarded. Her hair was falling in a tangle of waves around her shoulders, and she was wearing denim jeans and a soft blue sweater that clung to her every curve. He felt his body stir, and he hated himself and her for his weakness. With a supreme effort of will he forced himself to relax. It was almost over. After tonight he would be free of Lucy and would never have to see her again. So why was he not relieved?

His mouth hardened along with his resolve. 'Yes, go,' he snapped. 'I'll see you in the hall at seven—and wear something appropriate. The black you wore the other night will do.' And, picking up the photos, he strolled over to the desk and returned them to the drawer.

What did he think she would do? Lucy wondered. Turn up in a pair of shorts and a shirt? For a second she was tempted, but quickly dismissed the idea and walked out of the study. She owed it to herself not to disgrace the Steadman name.

Contrary to what Lorenzo seemed to think, she had been well brought up. She had attended a prestigious boarding school and art college. Her family had been reasonably wealthy by any standards, and their home—while not as spectacular as this—lovely. Not overflowing with staff, but there had been a housekeeper who'd arrived at eight every morning and left at four.

Her husband had been the gardener, and the acres of grounds had been well tended. When her parents had entertained extra staff had been hired. Her mother had been a beautiful, loving and elegant lady, whom everyone had adored—especially Lucy. But everything had changed after her mother died.

No, she wasn't going to dwell in the past—she had done too much of that already. And, flicking her wayward hair back, she ran up the stairs to her room.

Lucy stopped at the top of the stairs and drew in a long, steadying breath. The huge hall looked more like a ballroom, with exquisite floral arrangements and a small raised platform at one side, where a quartet were arranging their music. Already quite a few guests had arrived, the men all wearing tuxedos and the woman glamorous in designer gowns, some short, some long, and all probably costing a fortune.

Suddenly Lucy was really glad that she had at the last minute packed the dress the Contessa had given her. It was perfectly appropriate for this sophisticated party. And no way was she wearing the black dress Lorenzo had suggested. After this afternoon, she was never doing anything he said again.

The dress was by an Italian designer, and a classic mini from the nineteen-sixties. Not too short, ending two inches above her knees, it had a curved neckline that revealed the upper swell of her breasts and skimmed perfectly over her hips and thighs. But it was the fabric that made it sensational—a fine silk jersey almost completely covered in white sequins from neck to hem, except for the dazzling psychedelic pattern of silver sequins down the front. On her feet she wore high-heeled sequined shoes.

Lucy made it down the stairs without stumbling, and heaved a sigh of relief when she got to the bottom safely and glanced around. Lorenzo was walking towards her, his dark eyes blazing. Whether he was angry or something else, she didn't know. She had seen him conservatively and casually dressed, but wearing a black tuxedo, a white dress shirt and bow-tie he looked more stunningly attractive than any man had a right to, she thought helplessly, unable to take her eyes off him.

'You are late,' Lorenzo said.

He had watched Lucy walk down the stairs, a shimmering vision in white and silver, and she took his breath away. Her hair was swept up into a swirl on top of her head, with a few long tendrils left to fall down the back of her neck and either side of her face. She was wearing make-up, understated but perfect, and her big green eyes fringed with thick curling lashes looked even larger somehow. Her lips were a glossy deep pink that made him want to taste them—taste her. *No, not any more,* he reminded himself.

'Sorry,' Lucy murmured, and raised her eyes to his. She saw the desire, the hunger he could not disguise, and knew hers were conveying the same emotion. She caught the hint of regret before the shutters came down and Lorenzo spoke.

'Very eye-catching dress, but what happened to the black I suggested?' he demanded, and offered her his arm.

Consigned to the bin, along with all her foolish hopes, Lucy thought bitterly, and took his arm, thankful that tonight was the last act of this ridiculous drama.

They joined his mother, Anna hugged and kissed her, and Lucy lost count of the number of people she was introduced to. Teresa Lanza almost squeezed the air out of her and most of the other guests seemed very pleasant.

Then suddenly there was a hush, and Lucy watched as a stunning, tall and dark-haired woman in red on the arm of a much younger man made an entrance, pausing and looking haughtily around for a second or two.

Lucy felt Lorenzo tense beside her, and caught the slight frown on Anna's face as the couple walked over.

Anna introduced the pair of them to Lucy. 'Signora Olivia Paglia and her son Paolo.'

With the briefest of acknowledgments in her direction, Olivia wrapped her arms around Lorenzo's neck and kissed him on both cheeks. It would have been his mouth if he had not moved his head, Lucy thought, her gaze flickering between the two of them as the woman began speaking.

She gathered from her limited understanding of Italian that Olivia was reminding him of his friend, and how much her poor disabled Fedrico would have loved to be here. It was not possible any more, and it was hard for her on her own, but how grateful she was for Lorenzo's support.

Was Lorenzo really that clueless about what Olivia was doing? Lucy wondered. The only person Olivia was interested in was Lorenzo. It was blindingly obvious. She was playing on his sympathy for his friend with the hope of moving on to him. Or maybe she already had, if the rumoured affair the Contessa had told her of was to be believed. Well, they looked about the same age, and they obviously knew each other very well—they certainly had plenty to say to each other.

As if she wasn't hurting enough already, another thought struck her. Maybe the reason for Lorenzo insisting she meet his mother and play the lover had nothing to do with his fear of Anna contacting her but was a deliberate ploy to use Lucy as a smokescreen to deflect talk of his affair with his friend's wife. She wouldn't put anything past him, and it would explain why except for one lapse he wanted nothing to do with Lucy now she was in Italy.

She glanced at Anna, who was greeting someone else, and then back at Lorenzo and Olivia, who were still talking. She moved to one side, totally disgusted. Then she caught sight of the latest arrival, and a genuine smile slowly curved her lips as she walked forward to meet her.

'Contessa,' she said, and was greeted with a delighted laugh.

'Lucy!' The Contessa put her arms around her and kissed her on both cheeks, then stepped back. 'Let me look at you.'

Grinning, Lucy gave a twirl. 'What do you think? Does it suit me?'

'Perfectly—as I knew it would. You look lovely and it brings back so many happy memories for me. I was nineteen, and wore it the night I first met my husband. Now,' she said, taking Lucy's arm, 'come and show me this painting I've heard about.'

Lucy was happy and relieved to go along with the Contessa. 'It is on an easel in the lounge, I believe.' Arm in arm, they started to walk.

'Good—and later you can tell me what on earth you are doing with Lorenzo Zanelli. He is far too serious for you—though to be fair there is no doubting he is a very attractive man, and definitely all male. But be warned—he is the type of man a woman can enjoy making love with, but to talk with, to really know—never. He has too much pride and passion in his work. Everything else is on the periphery of his life, especially his women—and there must have been a few.'

'I guess so,' Lucy said. 'But I am not doing anything with him. I am going home tomorrow,' she stated as they approached the double doors. And if the Contessa noticed the hint of bitterness in her tone she did not remark on it.

Before they could walk through into the lounge, Lorenzo appeared.

'Contessa...' He spoke to her in Italian.

But she answered in English, with a mischievous glance at Lucy. 'No need to apologise, Lorenzo, for not greeting me on arrival. I could see you were occupied with Signora Paglia, and Lucy more than made up for your lapse.' As a put-down it was brilliant and she smiled at Lucy, her sparkling eyes brimming with merriment. 'Lucy is going to show me her latest work of art—shall we, dear?'

Lorenzo stood frozen to the spot and watched as the two petite women—one old, one young—both beauties, walked into the lounge, the sound of their laughter floating back to him. He had never been so elegantly dismissed in his life.

He was about to follow them when Olivia caught his arm again.

'Lorenzo, you never told me your little friend was an artist and had painted a portrait of your brother—how sweet. And she looks very sweet in that vintage dress. But secondhand clothes have never appealed to me—I prefer new.'

He looked at the tall brunette hanging on his arm. 'What do you mean?'

'Didn't you know? The Contessa gave Lucy the dress

she is wearing. Teresa Lanza overheard them talking, and apparently the Contessa wore it the first time she met her husband. Heaven knows how many years ago *that* was, but at least it saved you having to buy one for your mother's little *protégée*. She probably had nothing suitable for an occasion like this.'

Olivia really was a bitch, Lorenzo finally realised, and from now on Fedrico was going to have to look after his own business affairs. Disabled or not, there was nothing wrong with the man's brain.

Shrugging off her arm, he said, 'Excuse me,' and strode into the lounge.

He spotted Lucy with the Contessa, sitting on a sofa with a group of people standing around them. Lucy was laughing at something young Paolo Paglia had said. Lorenzo took a glass of champagne from a passing waiter and walked over to the group.

'Champagne, Lucy?'

Lucy heard Lorenzo's voice, though she had not seen him approach, and her smile dimmed as she looked up at him and took the glass he offered. If his interest in her had been genuine, and he'd seen her as more than just a body in his bed, he might have noticed she never drank the stuff.

She listened as he effortlessly joined the conversation. But his very presence so close was affecting her hard-won poise—and it was getting worse.

For a man who could hardly wait to get rid of her, and was prepared to pay to do so, he had an odd way of showing it, Lucy thought two hours later. Lorenzo had insisted on sticking with the Contessa and Lucy. He had totally charmed the Contessa, and kept touching Lucy—her arm, her waist. She knew it was just for show, but by the time he escorted them to the buffet laid out in the dining room she was beginning to wonder...

The Contessa left after the buffet, and the band began to play.

Lorenzo led Lucy on to the dance floor and took her in his arms. For a moment it was like the first time they'd danced together—a perfect fit. Held close against his long body, Lucy stopped wondering, and her soft heart began to hope...

Then Lorenzo burst her bubble by speaking.

'Did you hope to insult me by wearing the gown the Contessa gave you?'

It was like a douche of ice water over her head.

'Did I succeed?' Lucy asked, stiffening in his arms.

His dark eyes clashed with hers, something moving in the inky depths. 'Not really—it looks beautiful. But if you wanted a new dress you had only to ask. I would have bought you as many as you like.'

'I think you have paid quite enough already to get me here,' she said. 'As have I. And isn't it time you mingled with your other guests?'

'You are right,' he agreed. 'Maybe I *have* been a little neglectful.' And he led her off the dance floor and through into the lounge, where Anna sat with a few friends.

'Watch what you say,' Lorenzo murmured as he led her over and she sat down beside Anna on the sofa.

The doctor made way for her with a smile and, perching on the cushioned arm. Lorenzo said a few words to the small group which made them smile.

Lucy managed not to flinch as he finally glanced down at her and she recognised the familiar ruthlessness in the tight line of his mouth.

'I'll see you later, *cara*.'

The indifference in his eyes chilled her to the bone. She watched as he walked back into the hall and saw he was quickly surrounded by a crowd of sophisticated friends, all laughing and talking—including Olivia Paglia, competing with the rest for Lorenzo's attention. She looked as if she was winning.

Lucy turned her head away and, pinning a smile on her face, listened as Anna introduced her to Luigi, a small dark man, obviously Italian, but whose English was faultless—as was almost everyone's here, she thought. But then at this level of society that was probably to be expected.

'My congratulations, Lucy. Your portrait of Antonio is amazing—especially for someone so young,' said Luigi.

'Thank you.' She smiled, and when he said he was an art historian the conversation flowed.

For the remainder of the evening Lucy stayed where she was, only moving after Luigi rose to take his leave, kissing both Lucy and Anna goodnight. Then Anna excused herself, as it was nearly midnight and time for her to retire. The rest of the group stood up.

Anna kissed Lucy on the cheek. 'It was good of you, my dear, to spend so much time with us oldies. Now, come—I will find that formidable son of mine and tell him he has played host long enough. I will say goodnight, then you two can enjoy yourselves.'

Lucy didn't think so, but she had no choice but to follow Anna into the grand hall. Lorenzo's dark head bent towards his mother as they said goodnight and then Anna moved towards the stairs.

Lucy was left standing like a lemon, wishing she was

anywhere else but here. She could feel Lorenzo looking down at her, and reluctantly glanced up.

'Are you enjoying the party, Lucy?' he asked, but his eyes were still dark pools, no glimmer of interest in their depths. 'You seem to have been a big hit with everyone—especially Luigi…a good man to know in your line of work.'

Then just behind her she heard a young man's voice.

'At last the lovely Lucy has joined the dance.'

She felt an arm slip around her waist, and quickly pulled away. Another arm wrapped around her—this time Lorenzo's—and she heard the laughter of the people around, and a mocking, 'Well held, Lorenzo.'

'Careful, *cara*.' He smiled. 'Paolo is only a boy.'

But there was no amusement in the dark eyes staring coldly down into hers.

'I can see that,' said Lucy, her cheeks burning and her green eyes sparkling up at him 'Excuse me a moment.'

She spun out of Lorenzo's grasp and swiftly moved through the crowd, making her way upstairs without a backward glance. She had been ignored, laughed at and mocked, and she had finally had enough of the injustice of it all.

Kicking off her shoes, she picked them up and made her way to the bathroom. She stripped off her clothes and washed her face and unpinned her hair. Then, wrapping a towel around her body, she crossed to the dressing room and found her suitcase. She began to pack.

Carefully she wrapped the dress she had worn for the party in tissue. It was a beautiful gift from a lovely lady, though Lucy doubted she would ever wear it again. She left out jeans and a sweater to wear when she left.

She wanted nothing and no one to delay her departure, and if she didn't meet the usual designer-clad elegant standard of the ladies Lorenzo usually transported in his private jet, she didn't give a damn!

She walked back into the bedroom and, switching on the bedside light clicked off the main one. Dropping the towel, she climbed wearily onto the big bed. She pulled the satin and lace cover over her and laid her head down on the plump pillows. It was comfortable, and she heaved a deep, heartfelt sigh. This time tomorrow she would be at home in her own bed, all her problems solved, financially solvent, and free...

She should be ecstatic, so why did she feel so hurt, so defeated? She knew the answer. After Lorenzo's outburst this afternoon she had recognised at last the implacability of his contempt for her. Was it possible to desire someone and hate them at the same time? Yes, she thought bitterly. Lorenzo could.

From the very beginning when she had felt they'd made love Lorenzo had felt...nothing... She moved her hand slowly over her naked body, remembering. Not strictly true... She thought of the dark desire, the passion in his black eyes, the need he could not hide when buried deep inside her.

Then she remembered his comment on Monday night. The only time his brain stopped working and planning was in a moment of intense sexual relief... The only time he stopped despising her... And then she knew she didn't care what proof he thought he had. She had suffered enough pain to last a lifetime because of him.

Her eyes filled with moisture; in a house full of people had never felt so alone in her life.

Turning, she buried her face in the pillow and gave way to grief for all those she had loved and lost, letting the tears fall. For her mother, her father, her brother—but most of all for the love she had never had and never would have from Lorenzo.

# CHAPTER TEN

LORENZO had watched Lucy ascend the stairs. He had been watching her all evening. It was crazy, he knew, and he had to stop. Even if she had not been the sister of a man he despised she was still not for him. She was too young. Paolo was nearer her age, but he'd had some nerve, trying to put his arm around her. For a second he had wanted to knock the cheeky young devil down.

He glanced around the room. The crowd was thinning fast—time to do his duty as host and see them all out. He was not a lover of parties at the best of times—especially in his home—but at least his mother had enjoyed herself.

Gianni was on hand to round up the stragglers, and an hour later only the doctor was still in the lounge, as he was staying the night.

He glanced around the empty hall and saw again in his mind's eye Lucy descending the stairs earlier, a vision in silver and white. Damn it! She was in his head again. She had been in his head for the best part of three months, and it had to stop. He had to forget her exquisite little body was curled up in bed a few metres above his head, despite the frustration coursing through him. The woman was driving him mad. The sooner he could stick her on the plane in the morning and forget he'd ever known her the better.

With the last guest gone, he strode into the salon. He was too tense to sleep, and spotted the doctor still seated on a sofa. He shrugged off his jacket and pulled off the bow-tie, crossing to the drinks cabinet and pouring cognac into two glasses. He handed one to the doctor and sat down in a chair opposite.

'Brilliant party, my boy.'

Lorenzo agreed, and automatically asked him about his mother's health.

'Nothing to worry about. Her blood pressure is fine, and Anna is better than she has been in years. Lucy has given her a new lease on life. You as well, Lorenzo, I shouldn't wonder. You are a very lucky man.' He beamed at him, sipping his glass of cognac, more than slightly drunk. 'That young woman of yours is a true gem— beautiful and talented, with a heart as big as a lion, loving and compassionate…maybe too compassionate for her own good. If I had been her doctor I don't think I'd have advised a teenager to do it.'

'Do what?' Lorenzo asked, draining his glass. He placed it on the low table and reclined back in his chair. Had Lucy had an abortion? he wondered cynically, knowing how the doctor felt about such a procedure, being deeply religious.

'Why—give one of her kidneys to her brother, of course.'

A rushing noise filled Lorenzo's head. The colour leached from his face, and he sat up straight and stared at the doctor with horrified eyes. 'Lucy did what? When?' he demanded in a hoarse voice.

'Surely you must know? When her brother returned to England—after the climbing accident. Apparently the Swiss clinic he spent a day in said he was naturally a bit exhausted, but fine, and discharged him. A couple of weeks later his own doctor and local hospital weren't much better, and three months later he ended up in the Hospital for Tropical Diseases in London. They finally diagnosed him as having a rare disease, probably picked up in South America at the beginning of the year, that attacked the kidneys. The only solution was a transplant. Lucy was a perfect match—not that it did much good. She told me her brother died last year.'

'Lucy...' Lorenzo groaned her name as the enormity of what she had done hit him. 'Will she be all right?' he asked, terrified of the answer.

'Yes, she is fine—very fit. One kidney is almost as good as two. I got her blood results this morning. No food poisoning—nothing wrong at all. Probably, as she said, the wine and too much rich food. She is a very sensible girl, who rarely drinks and watches what she eats. I think Anna was hoping Lucy might be pregnant, but she isn't—and she is not on the pill, either. Doesn't believe in putting anything in her body that is not necessary to her health—very wise.' He suddenly stopped and added belatedly, 'But I should not have told you—doctor-patient confidentiality and all that.' Rising to his feet, he said, 'Time I went to bed. Goodnight, Lorenzo.'

But Lorenzo didn't hear. He was fighting to breathe, his heart pounding in his chest as the full weight of what the doctor had revealed exploded in his mind. Lucy—his Lucy—with the laughing eyes and the brilliant smile. It would kill him if anything happened to her. And in that instant he knew he loved her—probably had from the day she'd walked into his office and he had kissed her.

A host of other memories flooded though his mind: their first night together, when he'd carried her upstairs and she'd given herself to him so willingly. For the first time in his life he'd lost control. He should have known then he loved her.

He remembered kissing the scar at the base of her spine and asking her how she'd got it the second night they were together—when, after the first rush of passion, they had made long, slow love...caressing, exploring and having fun together. She had said it was just a cut, and, so engrossed in what she was doing to him by then, he'd never queried her answer. Later that night he had delivered a cruel cut of his own, and he couldn't bear to think how brutal he had been.

He had actually accused her brother of manslaughter and ended their weekend affair with a ruthlessness as insulting to her as it was shaming to him. Groaning, he buried his head in his hands.

Lucy was never going to forgive him—how could she? He was the staid, arrogant banker she'd called him, who thought he was always right. She had tried to tell him this afternoon, when he'd shoved his so-called proof at her. She had accused him of seeing things in black and white and suggested her brother might have been weakened or passed out. But had he listened? No...

Lorenzo had no idea how long he sat there with every day of the last few months he'd spent with Lucy replaying in his mind—every word, every action. He had read somewhere that love was a kind of madness and, given the crazy way he had behaved since he'd met Lucy, he could believe it.

Finally he got to his feet, and with a steely glint of determination in his eyes walked upstairs. He hesitated for a second outside her bedroom, then opened the door and walked in.

He crossed to the bedside and stared down at where

she lay on her back, her beautiful face illuminated by the bedside light, her eyes closed peacefully in sleep. His conscience told him the way he had behaved towards her was despicable and he should leave now. Let her go home as planned, and get on with her life without him. But he was not that altruistic. What he wanted he fought tooth and nail to get—and he wanted her with a passion, a depth of love, he had never imagined possible. Just the thought of never seeing her again tore him apart.

She stirred slightly.

'Lucy.' He said her name and sat down on the side of the bed. 'Lucy...' he said again, and raised his hand to rest it on her shoulder.

Somewhere in her dreams Lucy heard Lorenzo call her name, and her eyelashes fluttered. She moaned a soft, low sound—'Lorenzo...' Her lips parting in the beginning of a smile. Then she heard it again, louder, and blinked. 'Lorenzo?' she repeated, and felt his touch. She opened her eyes. This was no dream—he was sitting on her bed. 'What are you doing here?' she demanded, knocking his hand away and scrambling back against the pillows, tugging the coverlet to her neck and suddenly very aware of her naked state.

'I had to see you—to talk to you—make sure—'

'Are you out of your mind?' she cried. 'It's the middle of the night.'

'Yes—out of my mind with loving you.'

Loving her...

Her green eyes opened wide. She had to be still dreaming. But, no—Lorenzo was there, larger than life, minus his jacket, his shirt open at the neck. His black hair looked as if he had run his hands through it a hundred times, and his face was grey, but it was the pain in his eyes that shocked her most.

'You look more like a man on death row than a man in love,' she tried to joke. She could not—would not—believe what he had said…

'Oh, Lucy,' he groaned. 'I might as well be if you don't believe me. I love you—it is not a joke.' And, reaching out, he curved his hands around her shoulders. 'The only joke is on me, for not realising sooner,' he said, staring down at her with haunted eyes. '*Dio,* I hope I am not too late.'

Lucy hung on to the coverlet as if her life depended on it and looked at him. This was a Lorenzo she had never seen before. Gone was the hard, emotionless man. She could see the desperation in his eyes, feel it in the unsteady hands that held her, and she could feel herself weakening, beginning to believe him… Her pulses were beating erratically beneath her skin, her heart pounding…

'I have sat downstairs for ages, wondering how to explain my actions…the appalling way I have behaved towards you since the day we met…and the only explanation I have is because I love you.'

Her heart squeezed inside her. 'That has to be the dumbest reason I have ever heard for declaring you love someone.' She wanted to believe him, but with a cynicism she had never had until she'd met him she said, 'What is this? Some ploy to get a farewell lay? Well, you are wasting your time. I know exactly how contemptuous you think I am—a promiscuous, greedy woman who can't help herself around men and who you can pay off. But you're wrong.'

She was angry—at herself for her body's instant response to his closeness, and at Lorenzo for doing this to her now, when she had finally resigned herself to their parting.

'I only ever had sex once in my life before you. As for your paying me off—that convoluted deal was all *your* doing. All I ever asked from you was for you to vote with me and not sell your shares to save my family firm. I ended up blackmailed into your bed. So excuse me if I don't believe you love me. Just leave me alone. I am packed and ready go.' And then she added, 'Try Olivia. I'm sure she will oblige—probably already has, according to rumour.'

He looked stunned. 'Rumour is completely unfounded. My relationship with Olivia Paglia is strictly business, and I will sue anyone who dares repeat it.' He sounded genuinely affronted. 'How the hell did *you* find out about the rumours?'

'I met you coming out of her apartment building, remember? The Contessa told me.'

'I thought better of the Contessa—she is not known as a gossip,' he said, and she saw disillusion in his dark eyes.

'In fairness,' Lucy began, 'the Contessa did not believe them—and now I think you should leave.'

Suddenly he pushed her back against the pillows and leaned over her, his face only inches away. She heard the heavy pounding of his heart—or was it hers?

'Damn it, Lucy, I don't care what you heard. I can't leave you alone, and you are not going anywhere. I know I don't deserve you, but I love you—I want you and I need you...' he stated, staring into her eyes and seeing the darkening pupils. 'Though you don't love me, you *do* want me,' he said, with some of his usual arrogance returning.

She stared back, her mouth going dry, her body heating beneath the pressure of his.

'No, I don't,' she lied, still afraid to believe his sudden avowal of love. 'I don't really know you and I don't trust you.'

'Lucy, you know me better than anyone—but I can't blame you for not trusting me.' He leant back a little, resting his forearms either side of her shoulders. 'I admit I was determined to think the worst of you, and sure I was right about your brother. I didn't know until the doctor told me tonight what you had done for him— donating a kidney. Have you any idea what that did to me?' he demanded his face grim. 'All I could think of was you on an operating table, risking your life for someone else, and it ripped my guts out. I have never been so afraid in my life for another person. I asked the doctor if you were all right. Because in that moment l knew I would not want to live in a world without you. I knew I loved you.' He lowered his head and brushed his lips against hers, and she saw the vulnerability in his dark eyes. 'You have got to believe me—listen to me. Lucy, please give me a chance.'

'All right,' she murmured—not that she had a choice, trapped in the cage formed by his broad chest and arms, but the *please* helped.

'I think I have loved you from the day you walked into my office wearing that horrible suit with your hair scraped back in a pleat. I kissed you—totally out of character for me. With hindsight I can see it was unfortunate that Manuel was the man I'd lunched with that day. He gave me the photographs I showed you this afternoon, and his opinion on the timescale, and I accepted his conclusion. He is a strong man, and like me has not much time for weakness, but now I don't know and I no longer care. The past is past. You say you don't know me, but you do, Lucy. I am the arrogant bastard you called me, and I very rarely change my mind, but

I did that day. I was considering voting with you on the deal, but I was so angry I changed my mind. Then, when I kissed you, I was so overwhelmingly attracted to you I nearly lost control and was embarrassed by it. I lashed out at you.' He laughed—a hollow sound.

'I actually thought I was having a mid-life crisis... But it wasn't—it was you. And I have been lashing out at you ever since. I used my perception of your brother as an excuse to believe you were as bad as I thought him to be in a crazy attempt to deny what was staring me in the face. I love you.'

Deep inside, Lucy felt the dead embers of hope burst into flame. She could see the sincerity in his eyes—hear it in every word he spoke.

'I swore I never wanted to see you again, and yet I came up with reasons to visit you—each one crazier than the last. I was jealous of my dead brother because it was obvious you'd liked him. I was even jealous of Gianni, the butler, when you walked into the dining room with him laughing. I've never seen Gianni laugh like that in his life. And tonight I could have knocked young Paolo down when he laid his hands on you. I was so jealous.' He ran a finger down her cheek. 'I know it is a lot to ask, but can you ever forgive me for the way I have treated you? At least try and forget? Forget the argument over our brothers and business? Forget everything that has happened these past months and give me a chance to prove I love you?'

Lucy looked at him. Lorenzo was jealous. She had not been mistaken. But he was better than most at hiding his feelings. She thought of how on that first night, when he had remonstrated with her about her security, it had given her hope at the time, and of other instances when he'd been protective of her. He said he didn't care what her brother might have done. Later she would tell him how her brother had passed out when he returned home, and the rest—but for now she decided to take a chance, a leap of faith, and believe him.

Her green eyes sparkled and a smile curved her lips. 'I'll give you a chance, but I don't want to forget *everything,* Lorenzo. Some parts were memorable and should be repeated,' she said, with a wriggle against him and a teasing flicker of her lashes. Lifting her hand, she swept back the hair from his brow.

He caught her wrist, his eyes tender and passionate as they met hers. 'Oh, I think I can arrange that,' he said, knowing exactly what she meant. 'But first there is something else,' he said in a husky, unsteady tone.

Lucy tensed, wondering what was coming next.

'I don't expect you to love me, but I want to take care of you—keep you. I know I can make you happy in bed, and maybe in time you will grow to love me if only you will let me try. Lucy, will you marry me?'

Lucy felt her heart swell to overflowing. She saw the vulnerability in his eyes as he waited for her answer— her proud, arrogant lover was unsure…nervous. Taking a deep breath, she said, 'You won't have to try—I do love you.' She saw the confusion, then the growing hope in his eyes. 'I have from the first time we made love. And, yes—I will marry you.'

'You do? You will?' Lorenzo looked shocked, then his dark eyes blazed with emotion and a hint of tears as he wrapped his arms around her, crushing her against his broad chest, and buried his face in the fragrant silken mass of her hair. 'You are sure?' he queried, and then his lips sought hers and he kissed her with achingly sweet tenderness and a love that stole her breath away.

He lifted his head. 'When?' he asked, and his dark eyes watched warily as he waited for her answer.

She realised her confident, powerful man was still uncertain. 'Whenever you like.' She smiled, all the love in her heart shining in her brilliant green eyes. 'The sooner the better,' she said, and finally let go of the coverlet and looped her arm around his neck. 'Do we *have* to wait for the wedding?' she teased.

'*Dio*, no—I can't wait,' Lorenzo groaned, his voice thick with emotion and a hunger that Lucy felt herself.

Taking her arm from his neck, he stripped off his shirt, his pants. Lucy's eyes followed his every move. This was what she wanted—what she yearned for—and as he gathered her in his arms she met the smouldering darkness of his gaze and arched into the hard warmth of his great body, her small hands caressing, her lips parting.

They melded together—heart to heart, mouth to mouth—in a kiss like no other, full of tenderness and longing, passion and love.

'Lorenzo…' she breathed, as his hands slid sensuously over her body and her own caressed his satin smooth skin. He filled up her senses, and with murmured words of love and groans of fervent need their bodies joined in the primeval dance of love, finally fusing together in surge after surge of pure ecstasy, two halves of a whole in perfect love.

'I can't find the words to tell you how you make me feel,' Lorenzo husked as they lay satiated in each other's arms. But he tried, with softly whispered endearments. He eased his weight away, but held her close to his long body, his hands gently stroking her back. 'I don't deserve you, Lucy, but I will never let you go—you are the colour in my life. You are beautiful inside and out.'

A long finger found the scar near the base of her spine. 'I can't believe you did this for your brother.'

'Yes, you can,' Lucy murmured. 'You would have done the same for yours if he'd needed it,' she said lazily as she surfaced from the sensual haze that surrounded her.

'You have more faith in me than I do myself.'

'Ah, but then I love you.' She pressed a kiss on his chest and he rolled over on his back, carrying her with him. And as the dawn of the new day crept through the windows the dance of love started all over again...

'What the hell?' Lorenzo swore as a loud crashing noise woke him. Keeping Lucy safe in the curve of his arm, he sat up.

The maid was standing three feet into the room, and she had dropped the coffee tray she had been carrying. Her face was scarlet, and Lorenzo could understand why as Lucy opened her eyes and smiled up at him, stroking her small hand across his stomach.

'I just need to feel you are real, Lorenzo, and know I wasn't dreaming last night.'

Then to add to the confusion his mother appeared in the doorway, fully dressed.

'What on earth has happened?' she demanded of the maid, and then looked across at the bed. 'Oh, Lorenzo—how could you?'

Lucy heard the voice and snatched her hand away from his stomach, blushing redder than the maid and trying to burrow down beneath the coverlet.

Lorenzo pulled her gently back up. 'Trust me, Lucy—that will look worse.' He grinned and tucked the coverlet under her, putting his arm around her shoulders before looking back across the room.

'Good morning, Mother,' he said, with all the confidence and panache a thirty-eight-year-old man could muster when for the first time in his life he had been caught in bed with a woman by his *mother*... 'I want you to be the first to know Lucy and I are getting married.'

His mother gasped, and then smiled, and was about to rush over.

'But can you save the congratulations and the clean-up until later? Lucy is a little shy right now.'

'Yes—yes, of course.'

The two women backed out of the room.

'As embarrassing moments go, that has to be the worst,' Lucy said.

'Not really. I should have expected something like that. From being a highly successful, staid and arrogant banker, in control of billions, who has never had any trouble with women in his life, this summer has seen women running rings around me. But, on the plus side, I have found the love of my life.' And, laughing out loud, he tipped Lucy back in his arms and kissed her soundly.

# EPILOGUE

LORENZO guided the car through the gates and up the drive, a smile on his face. Lucy had married him in the cathedral in Verona on a fine October day—a vision in white and a picture he would carry in his mind for ever. And eight months later their son Antonio had been born—conceived, Lucy was sure, on the night he'd proposed to her. Lorenzo had his doubts, but didn't argue with his wife. She had filled his life with laughter and love, and she collected friends as other people collected stamps. Last week had been Antonio's first birthday, and they had thrown a party for their friends, and his little friends and their families, with a funfair set up in the garden.

Today was Lorenzo's birthday. He had spent the last four days in New York and could not wait to get home and get Lucy alone. He loved his family, but sometimes a man just needed his wife—and he was hard with anticipation. He had it all planned. He was going to surprise Lucy and fly her to Venice, take her to the Hotel Cipriani, where he had booked a suite for the night. They could share an intimate dinner…just the two of them…

\* \* \*

Lucy combed Antonio's soft black hair. He had woken from his afternoon nap an hour ago, and was now dressed and ready for the party. She kissed his cheek and handed him to the nanny to take downstairs. She had not wanted a nanny but Lorenzo had insisted, saying if she wanted to continue with her art it made sense.

He was right. He had arranged for one of the tower rooms to be converted into a studio for her, but she still had the gallery and visited regularly and showed her work there. Elaine now ran it, with Miss Carr the temp—who, having gone full-time, had ended up marrying the woodcarver in residence, confirmed bachelor Leon. In fact all four of them were here now, and downstairs with Anna.

Lucy walked along to the master suite and quickly showered and dressed. Sometimes she had to pinch herself to believe how lucky she was. Lorenzo had made her the happiest woman in the world. She knew he loved her—he showed it in myriad ways—and he had given her a wonderful son she worshipped and adored. He was a great father. How she had ever thought he was staid and boring was inconceivable to her now.

When they'd married he had asked her where she wanted to live, saying he would buy or build her a house anywhere she chose. She'd chosen to live in the house by the lake with his mother. He'd been surprised, but had agreed. They stayed at the villa in Santa Margherita a lot of weekends, and already he was trying to teach Antonio to sail on a specially built boat in the swimming pool. She'd told him he was crazy—the baby had only just learnt to walk—but he'd just laughed and made love to her by the pool.

He still worked hard, and commuted to Verona daily. Sometimes he drove, but he had a new toy—a helicopter which he piloted himself. Tonight he was driving home, thank heaven, otherwise he would be back too soon and ruin her surprise.

Three months ago he had surprised *her.* They had gone to Dessington for the grand opening of the new development, and she had discovered he had bought her old home. She had auctioned it off and converted it into a hotel with James Morgan. Not an ordinary hotel, but a centre where cancer sufferers and their families could have a holiday. Lorenzo knew her mum had died of cancer, and James had done it for Samantha.

They two were arriving any minute, with their son Thomas, and with one last look at her reflection in the mirror Lucy dashed downstairs just in time to welcome them.

Lorenzo stopped the car under the portico, leapt out and dashed into the house—and stopped dead. A huge banner was strung around the balcony, with 'Happy Fortieth Birthday' written on it, and the hall was full of people. His dark eyes went unerringly to Lucy.

She was walking towards him, a brilliant smile on her face, her eyes sparkling with love and laughter. The gown she wore should have been censored, was his second thought. His first was *wow...* A shimmering gold, the dress had a halter-neck and no back, he noted, as she turned for a second to speak to someone, and the bodice plunged between her breasts—slightly larger now, since she had breastfed their son. It nipped in at her tiny waist, then fell smoothly over hips to her feet. And he was in danger of embarrassing himself—but then Lucy always had that effect on him.

She reached up and looped her arms around his

neck. 'Surprise, surprise—happy birthday, Lorenzo darling.'

He wrapped his arms around her and kissed her as the crowd started cheering. 'You will pay for this,' he murmured in her ear. 'I had plans for an intimate dinner for two in Venice. We have to communicate better—starting now.'

And then Antonio came, hurtling to his feet, and he picked his son up and spun him around, and kissed his mother on the cheek. Then he was shaking hands and greeting people, but he put a hand around Lucy's waist and kept her by his side as he made for the stairs, telling Gianni and various others that he needed to get changed. And huskily telling Lucy *she* was going to help him.

'Lorenzo, we can't,' Lucy said, eyeing him with loving amusement as he shed his suit and shirt, dropping them on the bed room floor as usual.

Wearing only boxers, he caught her to him. 'Yes, we can, Lucy. I love you more and more each day. You have given me a wonderful son and you have made me the happiest man in the world. But it has been four days, and right now I ache to be inside you.' And gathering her close, a hand curving around her nape, he kissed her long and deep, his fingers deftly loosening the halter-top.

Lucy closed her eyes. He was right. She could feel the passion, the desire vibrating between them, and when he slipped her dress down to pool at her feet and carried her to the bed she wanted him with a hunger that could not be denied. She always did and always would.

Later, she slipped off the bed and told Lorenzo to wait. She crossed to the dressing room and, taking the parcel she had hidden there, returned to the bed. 'Happy birthday,' she said, and handed him her gift.

Grinning, he ripped off the paper—and stopped, his dark eyes fixed on the painting. He stared for so long in silence, she began to worry.

'I thought it was time there was a portrait of you above the fireplace in the lounge, and your father's was relegated to the hall,' she said. 'But if it's not good enough...'

He turned his head, and she saw the moisture in his eyes. 'Good enough? It is magnificent—the best gift, after our son, you could possibly give me. The days... the hours you must have spent... I am humbled and flattered that you see me so well.' And, slipping the painting gently to the floor, he reached for her.

Lorenzo Zanelli's surprise fortieth birthday party was talked about for months afterwards in the homes of Verona—mainly because it had taken him three hours to get changed for the party, particularly as his wife was helping him!

## Coming Next Month

from **Harlequin Presents®**. Available April 26, 2011.

## Coming Next Month

from **Harlequin Presents® EXTRA**. Available May 10, 2011.

**Visit www.HarlequinInsideRomance.com
for more information on upcoming titles!**

# REQUEST YOUR FREE BOOKS!

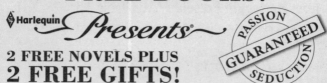

## 2 FREE NOVELS PLUS
## 2 FREE GIFTS!

*With an evil force hell-bent on destruction,*
*two enemies must unite to find a truth that turns*
*all-too-personal when passions collide.*

*Enjoy a sneak peek in Jenna Kernan's next installment*
*in her original* TRACKER *series, GHOST STALKER,*
*available in May, only from Harlequin Nocturne.*

"Who are you?" he snarled.

Jessie lifted her chin. "Your better."

His smile was cold. "Such arrogance could only come from a Niyanoka."

She nodded. "Why are you here?"

"I don't know." He glanced about her room. "I asked the birds to take me to a healer."

"And they have done so. Is that *all* you asked?"

"No. To lead them away from my friends." His eyes fluttered and she saw them roll over white.

Jessie straightened, preparing to flee, but he roused himself and mastered the momentary weakness. His eyes snapped open, locking on her.

Her heart hammered as she inched back.

"Lead who away?" she whispered, suddenly afraid of the answer.

"The ghosts. Nagi sent them to attack me so I would bring them to her."

The wolf must be deranged because Nagi did not send ghosts to attack living creatures. He captured the evil ones after their death if they refused to walk the Way of Souls, forcing them to face judgment.

"Her? The healer you seek is also female?"

"Michaela. She's Niyanoka, like you. The last Seer of Souls and Nagi wants her dead."

Jessie fell back to her seat on the carpet as the possibility of this ricocheted in her brain. Could it be true?

"Why should I believe you?" But she knew why. His black aura, the part that said he had been touched by death. Only a ghost could do that. But it made no sense.

Why would Nagi hunt one of her people and why would a Skinwalker want to protect her? She had been trained from birth to hate the Skinwalkers, to consider them a threat.

His intent blue eyes pinned her. Jessie felt her mouth go dry as she considered the impossible. Could the trickster be speaking the truth? Great Mystery, what evil was this?

She stared in astonishment. There was only one way to find her answers. But she had never even met a Skinwalker before and so did not even know if they dreamed.

But if he dreamed, she would have her chance to learn the truth.

*Look for GHOST STALKER by Jenna Kernan,
available May only from Harlequin Nocturne,
wherever books and ebooks are sold.*

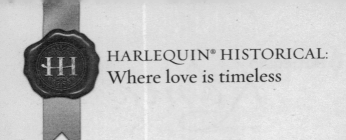

HARLEQUIN® HISTORICAL:
Where love is timeless

# Claimed by the Highlander

FROM FAN-FAVOURITE AUTHOR

# MICHELLE WILLINGHAM

### SCOTLAND, 1305

Warrior Bram MacKinloch returns to the Scottish Highlands to retrieve his bride—and the dowry that will pay for his brother's freedom.

His wayward wife, Nairna MacPherson, hopes for an annulment from her estranged husband who has spent most of their marriage in prison.

But the boy she married years ago has been irrevocably changed by his captivity. His body is scarred, nightmares disturb his sleep, but most alarming of all is *her* overwhelming desire to kiss every inch of his battle-honed body....

**Available from Harlequin® Historical**
**May 2011**

*Look out for more from the MacKinloch clan coming soon!*

A *Romance* FOR EVERY MOOD™

www.eHarlequin.com

HH29642